Sapplehead

K.B. Ross

Published by Haynes Publications, 2021.

SAPPLEHEAD

First edition. December 29, 2021.

ISBN: 979-8201577278

Written by K.B. Ross.

Table of Contents

Chapter 1

Sandy Templeton gasped as she glanced into the rear view mirror of her compact car. Her blue eyes widened as a dark sedan filled the looking glass. "I don't have the brooch they're looking for. Why are they following me?" Her long slim fingers grasped the steering wheel so tightly her arms ached, and the palms of her hands felt wet. She swallowed a lump in her throat and as she brought her attention back to the road, her breath burst from her throat in short sobs.

The trip seemed to be lasting forever although she traveled this route many times from where she was teaching in Colorado Springs to Fort Collins then on to Laramie where her grandfather and father ranched west of the gem city. But today she was rushing to her grandfather's funeral and the car behind her added to her stress.

In Fort Collins she darted down alleys hoping to evade her pursuers. On one diversion, she lost them as they zipped past her hiding place. She sat back in the seat and sighed. She had been taken in by the tall handsome John Sterling when he came to her apartment, but all he wanted was a brooch he said belonged to his family and was given to her grandfather's father when he left England years ago.

She knew of no brooch. They obviously had the wrong person, and they were interested in some other family. Shaking her head and angrily pounding the steering wheel, she pulled from the alley and headed for the highway leading to Laramie. "The old liars," she breathed. "There's no brooch and why would they want the thing after all these years?" Her teeth ground together, and she growled deep in her throat then her eyes brightened as a thought popped into her head. "Danny," she said. The retarded man who took care of their cabin would know the truth. "Grandpa could tell him anything because he always kept Grandpa's secrets to himself."

She glanced at the mirror again and sighed as the dark car did not appear behind her. A gravel road heading north caught her attention and Sandy swerved the car onto it thinking this last evasive move would leave John Sterling and his fat friend, Livingstone, far behind.

The sun gleamed close to the western mountains and Sandy guessed she had perhaps three hours or so before it set. A large dark bottomed thunderhead moved slowly from behind the hills and pushed its way across the early June sky, but she felt confident that before the cloud emptied its contents, this gavel road, winding northward, would take her to the interstate stretching between Cheyenne and Laramie. Leaning back in the seat, she sighed and let the air from her lungs serge through her lips in a whistle of relief.

Automatically her gaze darted to the mirror and a lump jumped from her chest to her throat. Dust from behind assured her that Sterling had found her trail. She tensed again and pushed on the foot feed.

"Oh boy," she breathed in terror. "And here I sit in the middle of nowhere."

Her gaze darted from left to right at the small farms and ranches dotting the edges of the gravel. She sped on, her gray pumps pressing the accelerator. Eyeing a plain dirt road, she dived onto it, the rear end of her compact spewing gravel as she turned.

Before her a large cloud of dust appeared. She gasped at the herd of cattle being driven down the dusty road by men on horseback and coughed at the dirt filtering into her car as she approached the herd. Her heart thumped loudly, and she licked her dry lips as she saw her escape route blocked and Sterling's car approaching.

Sandy's heart beat frantically inside the pale blue cotton blouse. What a situation, squeezed between a herd of cattle stretching out on either side of the road and Sterling behind. She wished she had the brooch they wanted, for gladly she would hand it over. Why in the world would they think she had it? And why was it so important?

She pushed the car horn, remembering what Grandpa did to make a trail through the herd, but the cattle only turned and looked at her. Finally, they started to move aside, and Sandy smiled weakly at her good fortune.

A quick glance in the mirror gave her more assurance. The herd filled the space behind, leaving Sterling beyond the cattle's broad brown backs. A strained chuckle escaped from her throat as she moved slowly forward.

Above the herd's bellowing she heard Sterling's car horn, but the sight of the men was lost in the dust and the cattle moving as a stream around her. Sandy gasped as something mingled with the dust. Steam began billowing from beneath the compact's hood covering the windshield with moisture then mud. She anxiously groped to find the wipers as the car began to cough and sputter. The lump in her throat enlarged and she growled with anger as the car's motor stopped, leaving her sitting still, the herd moving around her like a stream of dark water.

The last of the herd stepped around Sandy's stalled compact revealing the hood of the dark car behind her. She twisted the key in the ignition again and again, stomping on the gas petal as she urged the car to start. "Come on, you old thing. Start. Oh, please start." Exhausted at trying, she pounded on the steering wheel, trying to hold back tears of panic burning in her eyes.

Behind her, she saw Sterling slide from the driver's seat and slowly step out carefully closing the door as if enjoying the panic in the compact.

Sandy desperately locked her door and squirmed to secure the other three as Sterling smiling face appeared at the window. She watched the man pull on the door then look on the ground, searching as if he lost something. Sandy couldn't hold back the scream, seeing Sterling with a stone and knowing he intended breaking the window.

What could she do but scream although only Sterling could hear her? The horsemen were lost in the dust ahead and the ringing of the scream was confined to the walls of the tin box in which she sat.

Chapter 2

Sandy didn't notice the rider on horseback studying the scene from the tail end of the herd. The tall blond haired man tipped the large brimmed hat back on his head as he watched Sterling grab a large stone from the edge of the road. The cowboy spurred his sorrel as Sterling lifted the rock and let it fall against the compact's window. He heard the woman scream and dash out the passenger door then saw her fall as she tried to run from the car. With a rebel yell he headed the horse toward Sterling, ramming him with the horse's deep chest and sending him into the dirt. Then with one smooth action he turned from the man, leaned from the horse, and grabbed her slim waist, pulling her toward the saddle.

"Swing your leg over," he yelled. "I can't do all the work.'

Sandy felt a tinge of heat rising in her cheeks at the knight's smug retort, but quickly slid her leg over the horse and sat behind the curt man.

Sterling got to his feet and stormed toward them but stopped short as the heel of the cowboy's boot hit him on the chin. Once again he landed amid the sage and cow dung.

"Hang on now," the cowboy instructed as he headed his mount away from the scene and across the hilly grasslands.

Sandy clasped her hands around him and leaned her tear stained face against his broad back smelling of sweat, cattle and the horse beneath them. She chanced a glance behind, and her eyes widened as she saw the dark car coming toward them bumping over the clumps of sagebrush.

"Hurry," she shouted to the cowboy at the controls. "They're right behind us."

"Don't mind them," the man drawled. "Just hang on. You're rockin' the boat."

Sandy ebbed between anger and gratification for the smug man urging speed from the horse. Both feelings suddenly vanished, replaced by shock. She looked over the man's shoulder and saw the long legged horse racing toward a wire fence. Sandy whimpered, tightened her grasp on the man and hid her face in his back.

"Hang on," he shouted. "We're going over."

Sandy screamed as the sorrel left the ground. She felt the rushing air beneath her as she left the horse's broad back then groaned in pain as she slammed back into place when the hooves hit the dirt.

The man stopped, patted the horse's neck, and looked over his shoulder at her. "A jumpin' fool ain't he? You okay?"

Sandy tried to smile as she rubbed her bruised legs.

"Good," he said. "I don't know about myself. If that fence was one inch higher we'd all be eatin' dirt."

Sandy attempted to smile again but could only force a weak nod. Something told her this cowboy lacked something inherent to the breed. She knew ranch workers in her youth and this grinning, sharp tongued fellow didn't come from that family tree.

"Let's get out of here," she finally said as the cowboy gave the horse a kick.

"What did you do to make them so mad?" he asked as he headed the horse north.

"It's a long story," Sandy called into his ear. "You don't want to know." She hugged him tightly as they raced across the open land.

"I'd like to hear that story, but right now we're in a bit more trouble." He pointed toward the fence they jumped. "They're heading for the gate. Once through, it won't take long for them to catch us."

"Then go," Sandy said impatiently.

"Where?" came the man's irritated retort. "Where ya headed?"

"Laramie." She pointed to the range of mountains to the west of them. "I think it should be on the other side of those hills, if we're in Wyoming yet."

"If?" he asked disgustedly. "Don't you even know where you are?"

"Humph," she grunted. "Of course, I know. Well, I think I know. She gazed at the shock of blond hair sticking from beneath the sweat stained chocolate colored hat. "Don't you know?"

The Stetson shook back and forth testifying to his lack of knowledge about the land.

"I haven't been here very long," he confessed. Turning, he winked at her. "Have you?"

Disgust swelled inside her. Of course, she had. Then the years between then and now raced through her mind. She lived in Colorado Springs seven years, four years of college and three years teaching. Somehow those experiences away from the outdoor life she experienced as a child left her mind dulled. She must carefully pull back the outdoor skills her grandfather taught her; yank them from the dusty files of her memory.

"No," she finally said. "It's been a while since I lived here."

"Well," the man smiled from beneath the broad brim. "Seems we're two lost souls in a tight spot. They call me Dusty." He chuckled at something he failed to reveal and stuck his hand over his shoulder.

"Sandy," she said as she shook his hand. "I'm Sandy Templeton."

Before she could continue, Dusty leaned forward with laughter. "That's funny. Dusty and Sandy." He turned in the saddle. "Don't you think they go together?" He gazed at the blank look on her face. "You know, dust and sand. They're both dirt."

Sandy sighed. "Yes, I see. Very funny." She looked down the fence line. "But I think we'd better be going, or they'll stomp our dirt." She pointed at the dark car bumping toward them.

"Okay." Dusty's speech took a western drawl. "Hang on, gal. We're headin' for the hills." He spurred the horse and Sandy groaned at the forward movement of the sorrel.

Oh boy, she thought. *A comedian. All I need right now is a comic.* She glanced over her shoulder. "They're catching up," she screamed. "Do something."

"What do you want me to do, push a button and have this horse sprout wings?"

"Yes, if it would help," she snarled, seeing the car closing the distance between them.

"I'll accept any other suggestions," Dusty yelled over his shoulder then glanced at the sky. "Oh, oh, thunder. Sounds like we're in for a little rain."

Thunder peeled as they neared the hills covered with the protection of trees. Tiny silver drops of rain slid from the heavy thunderhead. Sandy ducked her head behind Dusty to word off the cold and wet.

"The trees," she shouted. "Head for the trees."

"The trees?" he asked. "You know how far away they are?"

"No," she admitted. "Then use your imagination. You can see where we're going better than I."

He turned the horse abruptly to the left down a rocky ravine and up the other side. He stopped behind a snow fence, watching the car attempt the rocky climb.

Sandy wiped the rain from her face and squeezed closer to Dusty for the warmth of his body and a little protection beneath the broad brim of his Stetson.

"I think we got 'em for the time being." Dusty pointed down the hill at the dark car grinding its wheels in the loose gravel. "They're pretty well stuck."

Sandy shivered behind him. "Then maybe we could find some shelter."

"Sure," he said. "Lots of gopher holes. Take your pick."

"Funny. Very funny." She helplessly pounded on his back.

"Okay, okay." He chuckled at the beating. "Let's see what we can find." He nudged the horse forward then stopped. "Hear that?"

"What? All I hear is the wind and rain."

"No. Listen." He pointed ahead of them.

"Sounds like cars on a highway." She looked over his shoulder. "Over the hill, maybe?"

"Certainly," Dusty smiled. "Over the hill, ma'am. Just over the hill."

The western drawl in his voice irritated Sandy. It didn't impress her at all. For that matter, nothing about Dusty appealed to her except his ability to handle the spirited animal beneath them. She pressed her head against his wet Levi jacket and glanced at the slim line of his denim thigh. Perhaps she was mistaken about this man. In this harried ride had she seen only an unpolished crudeness? Courage seemed nestled in his chest, and she rather enjoyed his uncommon sense of humor. She admired his adventurous spirit and a vulnerability that left him open to hurt. If this man felt anxious about the situation, he showed no signs, but urged the horse over the hill.

The interstate spread before them, wet, flat, and shiny. Only a few cars whizzed by toward the hills in the distance. Sandy watched them speed through the rain.

"Want to try thumbing a ride?" Dusty asked.

"It's against the law on the interstate isn't it?" Sandy tried to keep her teeth from chattering in the high country weather.

"You worried about the law at a time like this?" Dusty turned in the saddle. "You look like a drowned rat." He grinned as he kicked the horse's sides. "We'll go to the other side and see if we can't catch someone going west."

On the far side of the highway, Dusty dismounted. "Here," he said, handing her the reins. "You hold the horse. I'll try to flag someone down. Now don't run off and leave me here."

Sandy felt too cold and wet to reply. Night would soon slip around them, and she had miles to go before she could be comfortable again. As she watched cars zip past Dusty's outstretched thumb, another sight caught her attention. Across the interstate two men appeared to be watching them. Sandy felt the familiar lump rise in her throat.

"Dusty," she screamed from atop the horse. "They're coming again."

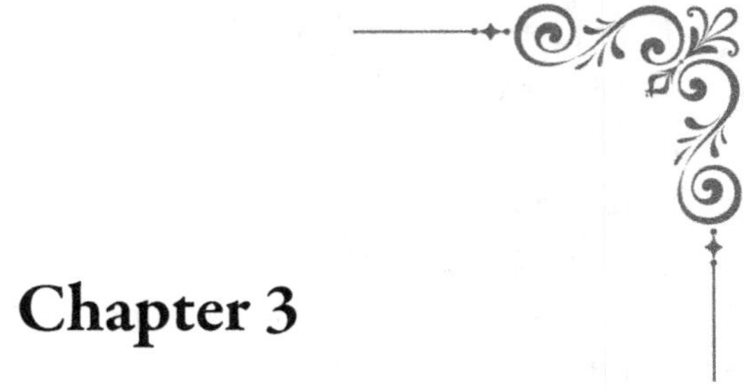

Chapter 3

Dusty stopped his thumb; half raised and vaulted into the damp saddle. "Are you sure? Maybe they're just highway workers." He jerked the horse's head toward a rocky outgrowth and gave the animal a kick.

"I'm not sure who they are, but shouldn't we stay near the highway?" She asked as she tightened her hold around his waist.

His broad brimmed hat shook back and forth. "You really mean that? You might want to stay, but I don't." He urged more speed from the horse. "Don't know why I get myself into these situations."

"Well, you could have left me. At least I may have been warm and dry," she grumbled as she hid her face against his wet back, trying to find some warmth from the chill wind.

Her words fell on deaf ears. Dusty either didn't hear or chose to ignore her sharp retort. He pulled at the broad brim to ward off the last of the moisture falling from the clearing sky now streaked with gold pulled by crimson ribbons tied securely behind the purple mountains.

Sandy looked longingly back toward the highway, its zooming cars appearing smaller as the horse galloped away from them. She wished for the warmth and dryness of the interior of her compact and a speedy trip to Laramie. Instead, discomfort and uncertainty loomed before her in the form of the Laramie Mountains; cold and dark and awesome. She should have insisted they follow the highway. At least they would know where they were.

The sun's afterglow, spreading a wide path across the sky, was pulled westward as the sun tugged on its ropes of light and rushed from the moon's pursuit across the heavens.

Sandy squirmed behind the saddle. "I have to get off. I can't stand it anymore. My legs are killing me."

Dusty motioned at the darkening sky. "Be dark soon. Don't want you wandering off and getting lost."

"We're already lost," she argued. "Let me down."

Dusty pulled the animal to a stop and Sandy slid from behind the saddle to the soft carpet of the forest. She stood a moment rubbing her sore buttocks then looked at the rider.

"You go on, I'll walk awhile."

Dusty hesitated a moment. "If that's the way you want it," he finally said as he gave the horse a kick. "Let me know if you change your mind."

She waved him on and began to walk behind him, stumbling on the wet, slippery rocks and tripping on the roots of the ancient trees. Her gray pumps were not the footwear for such a hike, and she knew it as she stumbled along trying to keep the horse in sight. Her blue skirt, dotted with mud, caught on the branches of the willow bushes as she forced herself forward. Her mind flashed back to her suitcase in the car stuffed with slacks, blouses, low heeled shoes, and a raincoat. Beyond that, she couldn't remember her purse that she slipped behind her feet, pushed against the front seat of her compact car. All her thinking consisted of the warm, dry comfortable clothes she left behind.

She pushed a damp curl from her forehead and gazed ahead. Seeing a long hill before her, she pulled a heavy sigh from her chest. Clambering up the hill, she groaned at the rocks tearing her stockings and the slippery surface forcing her backward more frequently than forward. As she reached for a rock to pull herself upward, her foot slipped and, screaming and gasping, she slid to the bottom landing in a puddle where the rain collected. Shaking with cold and anger, she sprang to her feet as the moisture seeped through her skirt.

Dusty didn't help her attitude by shouting from the summit. "You want a hand, or do you want to do it all by yourself?"

Sandy couldn't see his smile, but knew it spread across his boyish face. She scrambled up the hill grabbing rocks and branches, hoping to change the smile to a circle of surprise. The rocky surface of the summit was within sight, and she reached for another branch. As she pulled herself upward, the branch began to slip through her grasp. She felt the end of her lifeline and squealed; realizing another tumble down the hill awaited her. Before the fall began, Dusty grabbed her wrist and pulled her to the rocky summit.

"Thank you," she said timidly, brushing at the mud on her skirt.

"Feel like ridin' again?" he asked, a teasing smile on his face.

Reluctantly Sandy nodded, embarrassed at her own actions. "Yes, I believe I'm ready now."

Dusty helped her into the saddle and led the horse through the darkness.

The full moon poked its head above the eastern horizon and peered through the trees to the forest floor. The animals of nighttime ventured from their homes to feed and those of the light curled securely in their nooks to await the morning. None paid heed to the horse being lead westward through their moonlit yards.

Sandy's head nodded with the motion of the horse. She looked neither left nor right or forward, for her exhausted body forced her eyelids closed and her mind away from her surroundings.

Dusty's sudden yelp made her reluctant eyelids open.

"Hey, look," he called. "There's an old cabin. Shall we see if there's room at the inn?"

Sandy gazed at the wedge of moonlight illuminating the dilapidated structure before them. Half the rood had caved in, and its walls, grayed with age, sagged with the weight of time. Even in daylight the dwelling would have been invisible, but the moonlight, with its silvery spears, pointed out its hiding place.

Dusty helped her from the saddle and guided her toward the cabin's entrance. "Well, guess we don't have to knock. No door."

She smiled at his ability to lighten the heavy situation. Yes, he is like the cowhands on her grandfather's ranch. The same nonchalant attitude and the ability to laugh at any situation thrown at them. Perhaps her tiredness forced her to see in him the youthful, carefree spirit of the cowboy. And perhaps, now, with exhaustion, Sandy returned to the girl she had been. The girl who liked cowboys. She tried to shake the feeling back where it belonged, in her past, as she stepped into the dilapidated cabin.

"Not bad for the price," Dusty said, squinting into the darkness. He lit a match. "It'll do fine."

Sandy shivered and wrapped her arms around herself as Dusty piled pine needles and twigs to form a little mound, then struck a match to them.

"Don't you need some rocks around it to hold the fire in?" Sandy asked, wondering at his fire building talents.

He sheepishly gazed up at her. "Oh, is that how you do it?"

She giggled at his embarrassment and ran to get the rocks herself. No, he was not just like the cowhands on Grandfather's ranch. Hurriedly she assembled the stones around the dwindling blaze and babied the fire with more dry twigs then larger pieces of wood.

"Good one of us knows how to build a fire," Dusty said, backing from the blaze as warmth spread from the circle of stones.

"How did you live in a bunkhouse without knowing how to build a fire? They must be heated with gas now," she said, studying him closely.

Dusty chuckled low in his throat and sat cross legged against the log wall. "Yeah," he said. "They have gas now." He laid his Stetson on its crown and ran his fingers through his thick blond hair. "Actually, I'm not a cowboy. Not really. Just someone who studies them."

Sandy tossed more wood on the fire and stood closer to dry her clothes. She snapped her fingers and pointed at him. "I knew it. You didn't seem to be the sort. But the way you managed that horse, I thought you had to have worked on a ranch somewhere."

"Well, I do, but not for wages. I wanted to get some firsthand experience for a book I'm writing." He pulled his boots off and pushed them toward the heat.

"Then you're a writer. That's exciting." She turned her back to the fire and faced him, a tiny smile pulling at her mouth. "You certainly had me fooled."

Dusty pulled a blade of grass from the earthen floor of the cabin and placed it between his lips. "Always liked the animals. Rode them whenever I got the chance. Even joined a riding club outside my hometown. Someday I thought I'd like a ranch of my own. Maybe a horse ranch. Maybe someplace warm." He smiled. "If the book sells."

"Where's home?" Sandy asked, turning toward the fire again.

"Chicago," he said dryly. "This cowboy's from Chicago."

Sandy turned her face from him, hoping he wouldn't see the smile spreading across her face. "That's nice, that you can do what you want."

"Yeah." He grinned and a soft chuckle escaped from his throat. "Looks like I may have more plot than I bargained for." He pulled a flat stone beside the fire and sat on it. "How about you?" he asked. "You said you lived here."

"I lived with my father on grandfather's ranch, west of Laramie." She chuckled. "I wanted adventure and went to Colorado to teach school. I guess the adventure was right here after all."

"And those men, what do they have to do with all this?" Dusty pulled off his socks and gave them a shake.

"I wish I knew. They're looking for a brooch of some sort. They said they're cousins from England and this brooch belongs to them. They think I have it or know where it is." She shook her head. "I've no idea what it's all about." She shook her finger in the air. "But one thing I know. I'm going to find out."

Chapter 4

"Where are you going?" Sandy asked when Dusty headed for the open door.

"I'm going to get the saddle. I stuffed some sandwiches in the saddlebag."

He returned, dropped the saddle, and brought the leather bag to the fire. "Feel like eating a bit?" He handed her a smashed bologna sandwich wrapped in a small plastic container.

"Yes. I am hungry," she said as she took a bite. "Good," she said.

"And a little something to wash it down." Dusty drew a flask from the saddlebag.

Sandy sipped from the flask. "It's water," she exclaimed.

"What did you expect? Something stronger?"

"I just thought cowboys might have something stronger," she giggled.

"Not this one," he chuckled as she handed it to him, and he took a long drink. "Well then, are you heading to Laramie for a visit?"

"My grandfather died. I'm trying to get to the funeral on Friday."

"Oh, I'm sorry. It's only Tuesday. I hope we can get there by Friday." He wiggled his toes then pulled off his socks and gave then a shake.

Sandy tossed more wood on the fire and gazed across the blaze to Dusty. "Is your real name Dusty?"

"Not much of a cowboy name, huh? I'm Howard Davidson the Third. That's why they call me Dusty." He laughed and pointed at her. "Is your real name Sandy?"

"Sandra Mae Templeton the First," she said, tilting her chin upward and laughing. "And I like Dusty better, too." She yawned heavily in the warmth of the fire.

"So do I," he said. "We'd better get some sleep. We may have a bit of a ride tomorrow."

"Will we have to ride the horse to Laramie?" she asked as she laid close to the fire.

"Don't know. We can probably get a ride tomorrow."

Sandy didn't know if she believed him, but nodded, closed her eyes, and sighed as Dusty put his Levi jacket over her. Tomorrow she could find her bearings with the sun. It would be in the east and to get to the highway they must go south. Anyway, she thought so. Brushing a stone from beneath her, Sandy agreed with herself that the eastern born Dusty might not be much help, but at least she wasn't alone. At this moment she wished she'd grabbed her purse containing her cell phone.

Being alone didn't really appeal to her and being with a man might just put some fear into the men following them. And perhaps, just perhaps, Dusty had a talent for fighting off an enemy. He came from Chicago and her thoughts on that were street fighters, tough and rugged. The man lying beside her certainly must have some of these qualities. She slipped her body closer to him and felt his arm tighten around her waist. Her eyes closed with exhaustion, and she felt herself drifting into sleep.

As the full moon moved into the caverns of morning, Dusty pulled his arm from around Sandy and attempted to build the fire but failed. Growling, he stepped through the open door to see about the horse. He stopped short and his mouth dropped open at the sight of the broken bridle rein extending down the trunk of the tree.

"Where's the horse?" Sandy asked, staring through the open door.

"Don't know. He's gone. Must have bolted, broken the rein and got away."

"Well, this is fine. Just fine. Now we'll have to walk." She jammed her fists against her hips. "How could this mess get any worse?"

"I don't know that either, but it looks like we don't have much choice." He gazed at the timber. "Which way do you suggest?" When she didn't answer, but began walking, he followed her. "Oh, this way. Okay. Sounds fine to me."

Carefully Sandy picked her way around rocks and through tangled underbrush. She took care to keep her bearings by pointing out landmarks so not to retrace her steps. For all her attentiveness to the forest signs, they found themselves traveling in a wide circle. Sandy sighed and pounded on the tree she knew they'd passed before.

"Didn't seem this far on the horse," Dusty said, looking among the trees which hindered them from seeing far in any direction.

"We're not making much progress," she said. "We're traveling in circles."

Dusty snapped a worried look at her. "In circles? How can you even tell that?"

"This looks the same. Like we went this way before." She studied the timber.

Dusty shrugged his shoulders. "It all looks the same to me. I was hoping you knew how to get through this."

She sat on a stone protruding through the damp floor of the forest. "I was good at this at one time. I guess I thought it would all come back." She rubbed the morning chill from her arms. "I did just like Grandpa said. The sun is in the east. If we go this way it should be south."

Dusty studied the sky. "Sounds reasonable to me." He looked at her slumped on the rock. "Now that I know what to watch for, I can help a little. Let's try again."

Sandy slowly got to her feet. "You've never been in the woods like this before have you? Not even the Boy Scouts?"

Dusty grinned sheepishly. "No Boy Scouts. Not even much hiking experience in the woods, anyway."

"Humph," she grunted. "You're really a prize to be stuck with." Turning from him, she started through the timber once again.

Dusty shrugged and followed. "Can't expect us all to be Daniel Boone."

She ignored the curt retort and checked the sun's position as she pushed her way through the needled branches of the lodgepole pine. Accepting some of Dusty's suggestions, now and again, she ventured left or right, hoping he knew what he was doing.

The pines whispered with cool, soft breezes as the couple moved forward and the high country jays chirped and flashed their colors through the woods. Sandy, her blue skirt, and jacket mud spattered, paid no attention, but stumbled around rocks and pulled at willow branches that snagged her stockings as she passed.

Sandy finally stopped and breathed in the moist, perfumed air. Before her a rocky ravine dipped into the earth and huge boulders jutted from the walls. At the bottom a stream babbled, its waters accumulated behind a beaver's dam.

She stood silent for a moment listening through the noisy silence of the forest for a distant sound, one distinguishable from nature; the buzzing of manmade autos speeding down a dark ribbon that stretched from shore to shore.

Dusty stepped beside her. "Sure, we're going in the right direction?"

"Sh," she hushed him, holding up her hand for silence. "Listen."

Straining to hear beyond the sounds of the forest, she sifted through the sounds of a bee buzzing and the soft hum of the wind in the high pine branches.

A whirring sound carried on the wings of the wind, stopped, and then sounded again, mingling with the tranquility high above the crowns of the pines. It seemed out of place, as if invading the forest, and the wind, gently caressing the boughs of the evergreens, tried, unsuccessfully to clear the alien sound from its domain.

"What is it?" Dusty asked, and then his eyes brightened. "The interstate."

Sandy nodded and smiled at her own ingenuity. The sound of the traveling cars seemed to originate from across the ravine and perhaps the interstate spread just to the south of the hill opposite them. She gazed to the left and right hoping to see an easier route to the other side of the gash in the earth, but from her vantage point descending to the bottom seemed as easy here and anywhere.

"Want me to scout along the edge?" Dusty asked. "Maybe there's an easier way to get down." He motioned his arm up and down the ravine's edges.

Sandy's gaze followed his motioning arm then she shook her head. "We'd make better time going down here." She looked down the ravine's green, grassy floor, and the small stream meandering through its bottom. "It looks like easier walking when we get down there."

Dusty nodded. "Whatever. Let's do it."

Sandy took a step forward, but the heel of her gray pump stuck fast in the moist needle carpeted floor of the forest. Gasping, she felt her weight leaning toward the earth's depression just ahead. With all her strength, she tried to upright herself, but couldn't stop the pull from the bottom of the ravine.

She fell to her knees and felt herself begin to slide down the rocky ledge, the small stones giving way beneath her. Grabbing a branch of a young quaking aspen, she tried to stop herself, but it was Dusty, catching her from behind, who kept her from landing on the rocks below.

Quickly Dusty stepped forward and caught hold of the full blue skirt. He heard it tearing but kept pulling until the ripping sound stopped at her waistband.

Sandy reached her hand back to him and he quickly jerked her back to the high edge of the ravine.

"You okay?" he asked as he held her trembling body in his arms.

"Yes, I think so," she said, still trying to catch her breath. "Guess these shoes aren't the thing for mountain climbing."

"Sorry about your skirt. It's all I could get hold of," he said, shaking his head.

"Well, it couldn't be helped," she said as she tucked what she could of the skirt in the waistband.

"Okay then. I'll go first," Dusty suggested. "You hang onto me."

Sandy looked down the rock strewn edge of the ravine, then up the other side. "All right," she finally agreed and held his hand tightly as she stepped over the edge.

Dusty made his way around rocks, warning Sandy of loose gravel and slippery edges or stones hidden in the shadow of the tall grass as they carefully made their way to the sunlit meadow below. Tall grasses swayed between them and the steep hill they must climb, and Sandy stopped momentarily to quiet the shaking in her legs. Beneath her gray pumps water oozed from the soggy floor of the ravine and she squealed as the cold water reached her ankles.

"It looked dry from the top of the hill," she said as she leaned against Dusty. Lifting her foot, she gave it a shake. "I should have known," she grumbled. "These bottoms are always soggy."

"You want a lift across?" Dusty asked, watching her dump water from her shoe.

"No, it's ruined anyway." She slipped the soggy shoe onto her foot and waded a few more steps, the heels sticking into the mud beneath the tall grass. "Maybe I could use a hand," she finally told Dusty as she stood with her arms outstretched to keep her balance.

Dusty whisked her into his arms and carried her to the stream that fed the wetness of the grassy floor then put her down on the muddy bank. He gazed in either direction searching for an easy way to cross then he pointed down the river. "Looks like a place to cross down there."

Sandy looked at the natural bridge built by beavers to contain the stream and enabled them to construct their lodges. The dam of twigs and mud looked sturdy enough when first sighted, but as they approached the structure, it seemed flimsy, almost delicate.

Dusty stepped onto the branch constructed dam, testing its ability to bare his weight. "Seems okay," he said and turned to Sandy, extending his hand. "Come on."

Sandy looked at the bridge of branches and mud. On one side a small deep pond shimmered in the sun and on the other, water trickled through openings in the dam. Shaking her head, she hurriedly grasped Dusty's hand and began inching her way to the opposite shore. Branches extending through the dam's top hindered her progress and her heels continually caught in the mesh like surface of the structure. Grumbling, she finally pulled off the shoes and carried them in one hand, clinging to Dusty with the other.

One branch, protruding from the surface, became tangled around Sandy's torn skirt and she felt herself being pulled off balance toward the cold water in the pond. Squealing, she lunged for Dusty.

Quickly he grabbed her, but the gray pumps slipped from her hand, one falling into the pond and the other caught on the branches of the dam, then finally dropped into the water.

She sighed in disgust as she watched the shoes bob up and down then stop against the far bank.

Dusty pulled a branch from the dam and stretched it toward the shoes. Carefully he poked at one shoe, and then with long sweeping motions, he forced the shoe toward the edge of the dam. As the shoe came within reach, Sandy bent over on hands and knees, stretching toward the pond to secure the pump. As she touched it, the shoe sank beneath the water. She leaned forward even more and would have tumbled into the water if Dusty hadn't grabbed the torn skirt. Finally, she secured the shoe and watched him repeat the motion for the other one.

Sandy slipped her feet into the ill-fitting shoes and followed Dusty across the dam. As he turned to observe her progress, his boot crashed through the weakened edge of the dam and his foot lodged in the twisted mass of branches. Although he pulled to free his foot, the western boot stuck fast.

Sandy could not help but laugh at the man trying to free the boot. "Slip your foot out," she finally said. "Then pull the boot free."

He grunted at the grin on her face but tugged his foot from the boot then forced the boot from its prison. "All we need is for both of us to be without shoes," he grumbled as he pulled the boot onto his foot.

When they reached the opposite bank, Dusty helped her up the next steep incline. As they reached the top, Sandy dropped, exhausted at the foot of a tree. Dusty sat beside her, reached inside his shirt, and brought out a sandwich.

"There's one left. Care to share it?"

"Looks fine to me," she said, smiling at him.

The sun warmed them and as they munched the sandwich the breezes brought the buzzing of rubber tires on pavement.

Sandy felt her heart leap at the sound and giving her aching feet a shake, she forced her body upon the curled shoes. "My kingdom for a pair of sneakers," she said.

"Can't be far now," Dusty said, leading the way. "Sounds like those cars are right through those trees."

Chapter 5

As she rested, Sandy's mind flashed back to hiking in the woods with her grandfather, and his wisdom of the timbered hills.

"Sounds fool you," he used to say. "Something might seem close, when actually what you're hearing is miles away."

Sandy gulped the bite of sandwich as the memory surfaced in her mind. How she hoped Grandpa might be mistaken this time and the cars she heard were actually just beyond those trees.

Dusty clapped the crumbs from his hands and stood up. "That's the end of them," he said. "Our next meal should be in Laramie." He turned his attention to the buzzing in the distance. "Now, if we can just get someone to stop on the interstate."

Sandy rose from the stone and put her weight on the shoes. They felt as if they had shrunk in the sun's warmth, and she wiggled her toes inside them. "I hope that highway is as close as it sounds," she groaned as she hoppled after Dusty.

Through the trees she followed him, fighting the rocky surface beneath and the branches being flung at her in Dusty's wake, until they reached the summit of a hill and looked down into a grassy meadow.

Puzzled, Dusty shook his head. "I could have sworn it was right here." He listened intently. "Now it sounds like the cars are right over the next hill."

Sandy leaned against a tree, hope slipping from her mind. *Grandpa had to be right, didn't he? He couldn't be wrong this one time,* she thought as she gazed into the meadow dotted with sagebrush.

Her gaze followed the sage across the park to the trees on the other side. Squinting, she concentrated on something moving across the meadow then pulled on Dusty's jacket sleeve, pointing to the objects as she got his attention.

Dusty smiled. "Horses," he said. "And saddled. Suppose someone's having a picnic up here?"

"Looks like two of them." Sandy studied the scene. "Maybe we can borrow one."

"I'm for that," Dusty grinned as he trotted from the trees into the open meadow.

Sandy followed, hobbling quickly to keep up with the anxious man. The sagebrush tore at her snagged nylons and she pushed the tough branches as she raced through the sage after Dusty.

"I don't see anyone around," he said. "Which do you want, the black or the bay?"

Sandy looked at him in disbelief. "Which one? Does it matter?"

He grinned. "I like the black."

"Let's just do it," Sandy whispered, her gaze darting left and right for the horse's riders.

Dusty stepped quickly to the black and untied the reins when he heard giggling behind the trees. Curiously he peered around the willow stand and saw two nude bodies romping on a blanket warmed by a shaft of sunlight piercing through the branches of the lodge pole pine. He smiled at the scene then glanced back to Sandy. "They won't miss the horse," he said. "Come on."

Sandy stepped into the stirrup and was about to settle onto the leather seat when shouting drew her attention from the couple on the blanket to two men racing toward them.

"What do you think you're doing with our horses?" the men shouted.

Dusty looked at the men then at the nude couple on the blanket. His gaze finally settled on the red compact beyond the lovers. "Oh, boy," he groaned. "The horses don't belong to the love makers, but to the peeking Toms." He pulled Sandy from the saddle. "Come on. I read what they do to horse thieves."

Sandy hurriedly followed him to the trees nearby where Dusty peered back at the angry men, shaking their fists.

"We could have gotten away with the horse," she said, studying Dusty's fearful expression. "It'd been good enough for them, eyeing that couple like they were." She leaned against a tree, pulled off her shoe and rubbed her blistered foot.

He chuckled. "Yeah, probably so. We didn't know the couple drove the car and the peeping Toms rode the horses."

"That's true," she agreed as she moved her gaze from Dusty to her aching foot. Her eyes grew wide as she saw a small insect crawling up her ankle. "Oh," she gasped as she brushed the insect to the ground. "Wood ticks. I hate them." A shiver shot up her spine as she brushed at her torn skirt. "Now I'll feel them crawling on me all day."

Dusty grinned. "Suppose we should do a clothes check?"

She didn't ask him what he meant. Yes, she would like to strip and check for the pesky little suckers that found warm tight places to hook themselves as they, vampire like, drew their victim's blood. She shivered again at the thought of the tiny villains scampering beneath her clothing. "No," she finally said. "We have to get to the interstate. Checking will have to come later."

Dusty stepped lightly through the forest, a wide smile on his face. Sandy knew that he was thinking about checking for ticks later. The couple they left behind on the blanket sent a flash of heat through her and she knew he must feel it too. She shook of the feeling of desire as a sight beyond the trees brought her thoughts back to their goal. Cars sped on the interstate across the grassy plain ahead of them.

"Well, here we are," Dusty said. "Do you want to thumb, or do you want me to?" He grinned at her bedraggled appearance. "Maybe you should. How could anyone resist that lost puppy dog look?"

She poked at him with her fist, a playful punch, but Dusty grabbed her hand and pulled her to his chest. At first her thoughts flashed to the highway and the urgency to reach the ranch, but when she felt Dusty's warmth, she welcomed the closeness of the embrace.

Slowly and deliberately, Dusty slipped his hand under her chin, tipped her head back and kissed her full red lips.

Sandy's mind fled from the highway to the man holding her close beneath the sighing pines. With all her might she wished they, like the couple in the meadow, had been in the woods for reasons other than those that existed in their reality. She drew back from him, pulled by the necessity of the moment.

Dusty nodded in agreement, and they gave their attention to the interstate and dashed to the edge of the highway, sticking out their thumbs and hoping the travelers could see the urgency of their motion.

Sandy saw a large, black car approaching and started to smile then gasped. "Is that them? I think it's the men chasing me. We have to get out of here."

Dusty looked back toward the trees, his intention was to speed toward their protection, but Sandy pulled him across the highway and the median then bounded across the eastbound pavement.

"What are you doing?" Dusty pulled away from her. "We can't get to Laramie this way."

Sandy watched the black car speed down the westbound lane. "I think that was them. Maybe they'll have problems finding some place to get over here. I don't think there are many places to turn around."

"Are you sure it was them?" It could have been anyone. Did you actually see the men?" Dusty gazed down the highway at the car continuing its trek toward Laramie.

"No, I didn't actually see inside the car." Sandy said anxiously. "But it could have been."

"Now what?" Dusty sighed and jammed his fists to his sides.

"There," Sandy pointed down the road at a car as it slowed and stopped then she pulled Dusty toward it.

"They aren't going to Laramie," he argued. "Who knows? They may be going to Omaha."

"Who cares right now?" Sandy jerked the back door open and slipped across the seat. She smiled at the elderly couple in the front. "We really appreciate the ride," she told them.

"You looked like you really needed it," the white haired woman said. "What in the world happened to you?"

"Lost in the woods," Dusty spoke up as he slammed the door. "We need to get to Laramie."

The older man pulled the car onto the highway. "We're on our way to Cheyenne, but we'll be going back to Laramie later today. You're welcome to go back with us."

Sandy glanced through the rear window. "Cheyenne's fine," she said. "I have some friends there."

"You do?" Dusty asked as his face filled with hope.

"No," she whispered. "Well, I used to, but we have to go somewhere. I can't spend another night with those bugs." She rubbed at her waistband and her neck close to the hairline of her short, curly hair. "I feel them all over me."

Dusty checked the back window. "Well, I feel those guys all over us. I think we'd been better off running for the timber." He looked at the older couple in the front seat. "If those men are back there and they try something, these old folks with be in danger, too."

"Oh, boy," Sandy sighed. "I never thought of that." She slid forward in the seat. "There may be a car behind us trying to catch us. You may be in danger."

"Oh, really?" The driver checked his rear view mirror. "Well, we'll see about that." He urged more speed from the old Plymouth.

"Be careful, Harry," his wife warned.

A smile spread across the old man's face. "I can't turn down a little excitement, Emma," he told her as the car zipped down the highway, passed a truck, then Harry veered the car onto an off ramp. Quickly he parked under the interstate bridge.

"We'll just let them pass over us," he said smiling at the exciting chase. After a while, Harry slowly backed from their hiding place and drove back onto the interstate. "They may be waiting for us somewhere along the way," he said. "But it's not far to Cheyenne. They'll have to go some to get us." He urged all the power from the car's enormous motor and sped past car after car until Cheyenne was in sight.

Chapter 6

Sandy turned in the back seat and checked the traffic. Downtown Cheyenne always amazed her. She remembered traffic surging down Sixteenth Street but did not recall it being so heavy. Her grandfather brought Sandy and her sister Jackie here many times when they were children. After they did their shopping, Grandfather took them to the big western store. Every summer Sandy remembered getting new boots and jeans and long sleeved shirts with pearl buttons. The memory freshened in her mind as Harry parked in front of the same western store.

"This okay to drop you off?" he asked. "I think we've lost those guys chasing you."

Sandy smiled, thanked them, and slid from the seat. "We really appreciate this."

Emma poked her head out of the window. "We'll pick you up here about five o'clock. Be careful now."

Sandy thanked them again and led Dusty into the store filled with familiar odors of leather and new Levi's. She smiled at the arrangement of clothing, all as they had been years ago; the soft new Stetsons behind glass cases and smooth brown leather saddles straddling wooden horses. She felt she had stepped back in time. The years, months, days, and hours slipped back to her youth when the store's owner, a short balding man with twinkling eyes, stepped up to her.

"Sandy. Sandy Templeton," he said sticking out a small smooth hand. "It's been ages. I don't believe I've seen you since you were a child."

Sandy shook the small hand and smiled. "No. I moved to Colorado. Jackie, my sister, lives on the place outside of Laramie."

"Oh, yes. I know Jackie. She comes in now and again, but it seemed it was you that came in with your grandfather. I heard of his passing and I'm sorry he's gone." He looked her over from the fuzzy blond hair to the torn skirt. "But right now, it looks like I'd better take care of you." He shook his head. "Colorado hasn't done you too well."

Sandy shrugged and pulled the ripped skirt together. "We've had a few problems."

"Well, you came to the right place. Let's see," he said, studying her. "Looks like about size nine."

"Yes, but we have no money. You see, I lost my purse, and I really shouldn't buy anything."

"Your credit's good here. Always will be. You're a Templeton, aren't you?" He pulled slacks from a hanger. "Do you still like blue?"

"Yes, but I really shouldn't."

"No buts. Pick yourself out a shirt and you'd better change those shoes, too."

Sandy dressed in the new clothes and gazed at herself in the long mirror. "Well, yes. I guess I could send the bill to the ranch."

"Of course," the man said, smiling. "Just like always." He nodded toward Dusty. "And the fellow with you. He also looks in need of a change."

Sandy motioned for Dusty to pick out some new clothing. "Go ahead," she told him. "I think you've earned it."

Sandy picked out blue jeans and a checkered shirt, a pair of low heeled boots and a jacket with warm cotton lining. Perhaps Jackie would have something she could wear for the funeral.

The owner looked her over. "Now you belong here again." He reached into his pocket and drew out a few bills. "You said something about losing your purse. Looks like you could use a meal."

"Thank you so much for all of this. There's one more thing I could use. May I use your phone to call Jackie?"

"Of course. Right this way. You can use the phone in the office."

Sandy followed him to the office and dialed Jackie's number. No answer. "Wouldn't you know," she sighed. "She wouldn't be home." When she heard the answering service beep, she took a deep breath. "Hello, Jackie. This is Sandy. I've had a few problems getting there, but we should be in Laramie later today. I'll call you from there. I hope you can come and get us, and I'll tell you all about it then."

"Nobody was home," she told Dusty. "I'll try again when we reach Laramie."

"How about finding something to eat?" Dusty said as he rubbed his stomach. "I could really use a bite."

"Me too. Harry and Emma probably won't be back for a while."

Sandy thanked the owner again and she and Dusty walked down the street to a restaurant nearby. As they sat down, a young woman rushed up to them.

"Sandy Templeton," she said. "I'd know you anywhere. I'm Betty Gleason. Remember me? We played together when we were in school in Laramie." She sat down at their table chatting about their childhood years. "What are you doing back here? I thought you were in Colorado somewhere."

"Grandfather died and I'm on my way to the funeral, if we can ever get there. This is my friend, Dusty." She cleared her throat, deciding not to reveal the day's turmoil. "We had car trouble and we're having a time getting to Laramie."

"Oh, I'm sorry about your grandfather, but we're on our way back to Laramie after lunch." She motioned toward another table. "My husband and kids. I got married when we were still in school.

Remember? Well, we have to stop at Vetauwoo campground to pick up his folks. They're from Maine and camping in the wilds." She giggled. "We have plenty of room in the station wagon if you want a ride to Laramie right away."

Sandy wanted to decline and would have, but Dusty nudged her. "Let's go," he whispered.

"Alright," Sandy said reluctantly.

"As soon as you've finished come over to the table and join us. It takes us a little while to get things together." Betty left them as the waiter brought their meal.

"What about Harry and Emma?" Sandy asked as she bit into the hamburger.

"They'll figure out we've found another way to go," Dusty nodded as he evaluated the French fries.

After eating, Sandy and Dusty crawled into the back seat of the station wagon, the two boys; age's five and seven, climbed behind the back seat with a huge, hairy English sheep dog. She wanted to hurry Betty's husband, Dave, but instead sat back in the seat as the sheep dog behind her gave her a generous lap with his big wet tongue. She gave the enormous, hairy animal a shove as the boys giggled and tried to pull the large head away from her.

As the station wagon zipped down the familiar interstate, Dusty turned to look behind down the dark ribbon of highway but could only see the shaggy dog panting heavily. He rolled down the window and the dog promptly jumped to the seat beside him and stuck his head out the opening.

Dusty turned again and beyond the little boys making faces at him, he checked the oncoming traffic. "I don't see anything menacing," he said as he moved closer to her, giving the sheep dog room to sit by the window. He moved his arm to the back of the seat, around Sandy's shoulders as the boys began poking at her curls with a rubber snake.

Sandy cranked her window open a bit as the warmth of the afternoon poured into the car. Was it the weather or Dusty's arm around her that made the new clothes uncomfortable? She tried to push her thoughts to Laramie and the ranch, but the arm around her shoulders drew her thinking to the blond haired man sitting beside her holding onto his hat as the boys behind him tried to snatch it from his head. She smiled at the feeling that she wanted to be even closer to him. Shaking her head to clear the desire from her mind, she forced her thinking back to the purpose for the trip and sighed as she leaned against Dusty. She felt tired and dirty beneath the new clothes and began wishing for the comfort of a hot bath with mountains of bubbles tickling her chin.

As she daydreamed of the wet, warm bath, the sheep dog spied her open window and forced his massive, hairy body over Dusty and her.

"He always sits there," the seven year old said, leaning forward over the seat. "That's his place."

Disgust grew inside Sandy as she and Dusty moved across the seat giving the dog his place. Wiping the dog's saliva from her cheek, she sat closer to Dusty, the dog's tailless end wagging close to her shoulder.

Betty called over her shoulder for the boys to keep the dog seated with them behind the seat, but the boys ignored the warning, giving the dog a generous pat instead.

Sandy felt relieved as Dave turned at the Vetauwoo off ramp and followed the narrow, twisting road lined with trees. It seemed as though forever had passed as Sandy gazed at the large flat boulders stuck against the hillsides as if an artist had arranged them in a rocky mosaic. Vetauwoo had been a favorite place to picnic during the summers she spent with grandmother and grandfather. She didn't remember the history they had told her about this place only that the Native American word meant earth born spirit.

Dave eased the station wagon through the picnic sites and finally stopped beneath a huge boulder where an older couple sat at the picnic table laden with chips and dips and covered dishes. Smoke rose from the charcoal briquettes on the grill.

The boys and the dog scrambled from the car crawling over the seat to exit by the front doors. Sandy squeezed closer to Dusty as they jumped past her.

"Looks like we'll have a picnic with Dave's folks," Betty said as she opened the car door for them. "You just as well join us."

Sandy nodded slowly. There seemed nothing else to do. She stepped from the car and gazed at the familiar campsite. "Yes," she told Betty. "I guess we can eat with you." She looked at Dusty, adjusting his hat after the boy's mauling. "What do you think, Dusty?"

"Sounds good to me," Dusty said surveying the road. "Where do you think your friends are? The ones in the black car."

"Don't know. You don't suppose they've given up, do you?"

"We gave them a merry chase," Dusty said as he doctored his hamburger with mustard and catsup. "Depends on how bad they want whatever it is you don't have."

"I don't have that brooch or any brooch. Brooches are for old ladies. They'll have to go somewhere else to find their old brooch." She grabbed a hamburger and watched the boys feeding their sandwich to the dog.

"Makes you wonder if you want any of the little devils," Dusty said motioning toward the boys.

"Speaking of devils," Sandy said, pointing to a car moving down the road toward them. "I think that's them." Her heart leaped to her throat as she flashed a look at Dusty who was already moving toward the timber, stuffing the burger into his shirt front. Giving her own sandwich a yearning look, she quickly hurried after him. She felt her heart would explode beneath her gray jacket and she patted her chest, trying to sooth the throbbing muscle as she raced to the trees.

They stopped behind the dense cover of pines and the deadfall and shrubs that tried to hide the enormous stones protruding from their carpeted floor made sufficient cover for the couple.

Sandy puffed as she stood beside Dusty and gazed back toward the campsite. Panic flashed through her as she saw Dave pointing toward them. "Dave's giving us away," she whispered.

Chapter 7

Sandy and Dusty fled through the long shafts of sunlight piercing the carpeted floor and hop scotching among the trees. Dried branches snapped beneath their feet and neither tried to conceal their location by treading carefully on the dry undergrowth. Their path became an uphill climb and the hill before them, its boulders overlying one another, stopped their upward progress.

Sandy nervously bit at her lower lip as she gazed at the mountain of boulders before her then followed Dusty up the steep incline. Puffing behind a large flat boulder, she stopped, grasping her chest. "Let's stop here," she said, pointing to a cave like opening between the rocks.

Quickly she crawled into the rocky structure, Dusty following her. She lay close to his back, not being able to see out as Dusty filled the opening.

Dusty carefully reached inside his shirt and brought out the hamburger he stuffed there. "Want a bite?" he asked, handing the sandwich over his shoulder.

"How can you think of eating at a time like this?" she asked disgustedly.

"Looks like I'll need all the strength I can get." He grinned taking a bite. "Sure, you don't want some?"

She felt like pounding his back but shook her head. "My appetite is gone. I can't eat a thing." Anger began building in her chest at his nonchalant attitude. "Can't you ever be serious? Of all the men on earth, I have to be stuck out here with you."

"I am serious," he said. "Deadly serious." He took another bite. "It could be worse. You could be out here alone with those two goons."

"They're not goons, really. They're Englishmen."

"Well, English goons," he corrected himself. "But goons just the same." Lifting his hand for silence, he hushed her. "Sh, I thought I heard something. Our voices carry up here, you know."

Yes. She remembered long ago when she went with her grandfather, hearing the climbers on the rocks high above her as the family picnicked at the campground below. Hiding her face in Dusty's warm back, she waited in silence, hoping he only heard a deer leaping through the forest.

Hours seemed to pass and still they lay hidden in the crevice of the rock. Huge thunderheads formed on the mountains to the west and boiled higher as they drifted east toward the Summit and the rock where the young couple waited in silence. Thunder pealed and seemed to echo among the granite rocks of Vetauwoo as rain splattered on the giant stones surrounding their hiding place. Faster the drops fell from the darkened clouds until they ran in small streams down the smooth stones.

Dusty squeezed closer to Sandy as the tiny rivers invaded the crevice. He squealed at the water's coldness. "Maybe this'll stop those guys," he whispered over his shoulder. "These wet rocks look pretty slippery."

She nodded against his back then wiggled her foot, feeling numbness inside her boot. Giving it a shack, she felt circulation surge through her foot and a tingling begin. She didn't think she could lay against that cold stone any longer when she felt Dusty pull away from her and slide from the crevice.

"I think it's all over," he said. "Come on. Let's get out of here. I can't lay in that place any longer." He stood on the slippery rock, trying to keep his balance as he stretched.

"See anyone?" Sandy asked as she scooted out.

"Not a soul. I think the rain scared them off." He grabbed Sandy's hand as she stood up. "Careful. These rocks are slippery."

Sandy surveyed the rocks above and below as she clenched her toes inside her boots to hold herself upright on the large flat surface.

"I think they've probably gone," she said.

"That's what I said. The rain scared them off," he argued.

"So, you did," she said and started climbing the rock to the heights above.

The late afternoon sun shone on the summit as Sandy and Dusty reached the top of the massive pile of stones. She gazed down from her lofty perch and motioned for Dusty to look.

"There's the picnic ground. I don't see that car," she said. "Now all we have to do is climb down and get back to Betty and the boys."

"Are you sure they'll still be there?" Dusty asked. "It's been quite a while since we left them."

"I don't know," she shrugged. "But maybe they're not our only ride." She pointed to the voices directly below and smiled at the hikers climbing from the campground.

"Let's get down there," he urged.

Large flat stones also covered the descending side of the hill. Gray jays screamed from the trees growing between the rocks, and tiny striped ground squirrels scampered across the hard, wet surface of the stones.

Sandy eased down the boulder's broad face, but as she scooted on her rump and feet, the new boots slipped, and she found herself sliding toward the campground far below. Screaming, she tried to catch herself, but the smooth surface held nothing on which to cling. She felt herself sliding slowly, then faster toward the rocks below.

A sturdy pine stopped her, and she groaned as the tree caught between her legs. She lay against the stone gasping for breath then looked above as Dusty ran back and forth yelling for her to hang on. *Hang on?* She thought. *The tree is hanging on to me.*

She looked down, hoping she could descend the rock to safety, for the climb back to Dusty looked impossible. The lower edge of the rock sat embedded in the firm soil and formed a small path between it and the rock jutting out below her. She hung onto the tree and tried to lower herself to the path, daring not let go of the tree's strong branch for fear of being dashed against the stones as she landed.

Again, she gazed at Dusty, who lay on his stomach reaching toward her. Sandy used the branch to climb back to her original position and stretched herself upward toward Dusty until she felt his fingers.

"Try and take a step up," Dusty shouted. "I'll catch your hand."

Sandy looked at the tree trunk on which her feet rested. If she jumped far enough she might miss the tree coming back down and slide to her death. Shutting that from her mind, she took a deep breath and pushed against the tree with her feet, her eyes on Dusty's hand reaching out to grab her. She sprung from the tree's trunk and extended her arm toward Dusty. It seemed an eternity before Dusty grabbed her hand and another great length of time until she clasped his. She felt him grab the collar of her blue jacket and pull her to safety like a cat carrying her kitten.

As Sandy stood trembling on the summit, Dusty embraced her, holding her close. "We'll find a better way down," he said. "Maybe not as fast, but better."

She giggled at his joking and welcomed the warmth of its delivery. "Let's find that way down," she said. "We're almost home."

"It won't be long now," he reassured her. "It just can't be."

Chapter 8

Sandy led the way across the smooth stones, their sides streaked from ages of water running over their edges. She searched for an easy way down then pointed to climbers on the rocky hill west of them.

"Looks like they're walking on a path. Yes, I remember a path when Grandpa brought Jackie and me up here," she told Dusty.

Dusty fought the slippery rocks, holding on with only his will power. "I'm for a path," he said, darting a glance where she pointed. "Looks like easier going further down."

They slipped and slid, hanging onto the lodgepole and limber pine as they made their way along the rocky slope.

Sandy hopped from the edge of the bolder to a gravel path leading between the rocks. "There must be paths all over this hill," she said, welcoming the solid ground.

"I'm thankful for that," Dusty said as he jumped to the path. "Looks like they all end up at the campground."

Sandy nodded and began following the path that led between the rocks. As they approached a drop off the path ended but attached to the huge stone a flight of brown wooden steps clung and below the stairs the path continued.

"Now this is service," Dusty said as he followed Sandy down the sturdy steps.

"Yes," Sandy giggled. "Forest Service probably."

"Very funny," Dusty grinned. "I'm glad to see a sense of humor coming to the top." He touched her shoulder and pulled her toward him. "Smooth sailing the rest of the way down."

She welcomed the comfort and the drumming of his heart against her own. A sigh escaped from her lungs, and she longed to stay in his arms, but urgency forced her to push him away. "We have to get to Laramie and call Jackie," she said as she stepped away from him trying unsuccessfully to quiet the pounding in her chest.

Dusty shrugged then stuck his arm into the air. "Onward then. Brave Lancelot is once more rejected by the fair maiden, but does he sulk? Oh, my no. Onward he goes and onward."

Sandy giggled to herself. *He is cute*, she thought. *I'm really glad he's funny instead of grumbling about this. Yes, he does have some redeeming qualities.*

The path sneaked between the pines and squeezed among the great cracks in the rocks then finally divided, one going to their left and the other turned right.

Sandy sighed, gazing one way then the other. "They both look like they go back to the top."

"Well." Dusty placed his hands on his narrow hips. "Make a choice." He pointed toward the right. "We did see those people over this way."

"They both end at the campground, I'd think." She gazed in both directions again. "Let's try the left one."

"Sure." Dusty surveyed the hill again. "We could just slide down this rock. Looks like the path continues down there."

Sandy studied the stone below them and the water streaming down its surface. "Looks pretty wet to me," she said and continued to the left.

"Whatever," Dusty said, irritation in his voice.

The path followed downward but ended at a stony cliff which dropped off to chokecherry bushes below.

"Gee whiz," Dusty said as he gazed over the cliff. "You don't suppose we should have gone right, do you?"

Sandy felt an angry flush rising in her cheeks. Her decision was wrong, but he didn't have to make fun of her. "Humph," she grunted as she watched a tiny striped chipmunk scamper beside her boot and dart between the rocks. "We just have to go the other way, that's all." She stomped down the path, Dusty chuckling behind her and tapping her shoulder as he motioned to a sign close to the ground with an arrow pointing the way.

"So, I was wrong," she snapped. "What's the big deal about that?"

"None, none." Dusty backed up at her anger. "I just thought you knew all about this country."

"I did once." She stopped in the path and looked at him. "I'm sorry. Guess I've been a pain, huh?"

"You have good reason," he said gently and reached out for her and as she stepped toward him, he smoothed her fuzzy hair. "Yes, yes. Very good reason." He kissed her head then gently tipped her head back and kissed her warm lips.

Sandy let herself be swept into the moment of comfort, pushing the day's events aside as she accepted the warmth provided by the tall, lean, blond man.

"Thanks," she finally said. "I needed that."

Dusty cleared fullness from his throat. "I'm available anytime."

She reluctantly pulled from him and made her way down the well-worn path to the campsite. Several families watched them hop from the last stone and a very heavy set woman, tending steaks on a grill, smiled at them.

"We saw you slide from that rock up there," she said. "Thought you were a goner." She motioned for them to come to the table. "You'd better rest yourself awhile. That was quite an experience."

Sandy smiled at the warm welcome but declined the invitation. "We have to get to Laramie," she said. "We came with a friend and hopefully they're still here. We got caught in the rain up there." She pointed to the hill's rocky summit.

"Well, okay," the woman said as she turned the steaks. "If they went already, you come back here. We'll take you to Laramie."

Thankfulness swelled inside Sandy. "We really appreciate that. If our friends are gone, we'll be back." She and Dusty started down the narrow, winding, paved road leading to other picnic sites.

"Do you suppose they'd slap a couple more steaks on for us?" Dusty asked as he walked close to Sandy.

"I can't think of anything I'd like more right now," she said, her mouthwatering as the breeze brought the steak's aroma through the trees.

They checked each picnic spot along the way trying to remember just where they'd left Dave and Betty.

"It was under the edge of a big rock," Dusty reminded her. "There," he said, pointing down the trail.

They ran toward the stone jutting from the ground, but Betty and her family were gone. A young couple sat at the table drinking wine and gazing into each other's eyes.

Sandy shrugged. "Looks like we'll have to accept that woman's invitation."

"Hope the steaks are done," Dusty said, striding ahead of her.

She trotted after him to keep up. The aroma filling the air set off a grumbling in her stomach and she hurried to partake of something more than smells.

The woman smiled at their return. "I thought maybe you'd come back. That rain scared off a lot of them." She patted the table. "Sit down. My husband, Bill, here, and I will drive you to Laramie after we eat. I'm Maggie."

Bill, a thin, tall man scooted over to make room for the visitors. He said nothing but eyed them suspiciously.

Sandy dismissed the distrust in his eyes and hurriedly slid onto the picnic bench, all her attention directed to the steak before her. She didn't think meat ever tasted so good. The dark crispy edges and rather raw interior would, at one time, have been discouraging, but now she could hardly wait to get it cut to savor its tastefulness.

After cleaning up and packing the picnic supplies in their old blue pickup, Bill and Maggie squeezed close together to make room for Sandy and Dusty.

"A tight squeeze," Maggie chuckled. "But you can't get too much togetherness, I always say."

Sandy nodded, not being able to create enough breath to speak. She felt the softness of Maggie's large body as the pickup bounced over the narrow road. She looked at Dusty clinging to the outside edge of the ragged seat by the hip pockets of his Levi's.

"You two just passing through this country?" Bill asked as he leaned forward to see Sandy hidden in Maggie's rolls of flesh.

"Yeah," Dusty answered.

"No," Sandy said at the same time. She looked at Dusty and grinned. "Well, yes and no. He's passing through and I'm visiting in Laramie."

"Oh," Bill said and pulled his gaze from them back to the road.

My, how that must have sounded, Sandy thought. Any more explaining would probably get her into more trouble. The situation couldn't be explained easily and lying made it seem more ridiculous. She leaned her head back on the seat and watched the evening sky cloaked in scarlet and gold. One more day before Grandpa's funeral and the way things were going, she wondered if she'd arrive on time for the service. Sighing deeply, she let her eye lids close as the pickup rocked her to sleep pinned between Maggie's soft folds and Dusty's jabbing hip bone.

She woke suddenly as she felt a sharp object poke her. It was Dusty jabbing her with his elbow. "The man wants to know where to let us out," Dusty told her.

Sandy blinked the sleep from her eyes and saw Laramie out the windshield, its nightlights shining in the distance. She thought of a phone. She had to get to a phone. Her mind quickly laid out the streets of Laramie and the road to the ranch.

"How about just dropping us down town?" she said.

"Downtown?" Maggie asked. "Your family don't live downtown do they?"

"No," Sandy said quickly. "On a ranch west of town. I'll call them and they'll pick us up." She watched the thin Bill give his wife a look of disbelief.

They proceeded down the street, passing fast food chains along the town's entryway and Wyoming's university.

As they reached the main street, Sandy motioned for Bill to turn right. She gazed at the buildings, most of which had stood in these same locations since the town was new. It felt good to be home. Very good. As they went down the street, Sandy remembered when she and Grandpa stopped here and there. Yes, being home felt good.

"About where do you want out?" Bill asked as he stopped at a red traffic light.

Sandy searched down the street then pointed to the overpass stretching above the rails of the Union Pacific. "There, by the overpass," she said. "That's the way to the ranch, over the overpass. We can call Jackie from the little store on the corner."

Bill stopped the pickup by the small market, which sold gas and other items a customer might buy if in a hurry.

Sandy thanked them and stood beside Dusty as she gazed up and down the street. "Come on," she told him. "There's probably a pay phone inside." She followed Dusty into the market and searched the walls for a phone. When she saw none, she asked to use the store's private one.

※

As Sandy went into a small office at the back of the store, Dusty strode up and down the two short isles loaded with bread, potato chips and soft drinks. He pulled a cola from the cooler, paid for it, and stepped outside to drink it. He checked the big round clock through the window. Almost ten thirty. Perhaps this would be a good place to leave Sandy and hitch a ride back to Colorado.

She may need his help, though, he thought as he took another drink. And, too, he felt intrigued by the mystery unfolding here. Why would those men want an old brooch? He shook his head. None of it made sense and that enhanced his interest. It would eat on him forever if he didn't find out the mystery of that old brooch. Did it hold a secret? Well, of course it did, or they wouldn't want it. But why did they think Sandy had it? He shrugged. Maybe she actually had the brooch and wasn't saying anything. He shook his head, crushed the empty can with his hand, tossed it into a trash can and stepped back into the store.

"Oh, well," he breathed. "Just as well see this through."

Chapter 9

Sandy gazed around the small office as she waited for someone at the ranch to answer the phone. The mounted trout on the wall looked at her from an open plastic eye. She smiled, remembering going fishing with Grandpa at his cabin in the snowy mountains to the west. She was probably four or five years old and could still feel the spongy, wiggling worm Grandpa helped her force onto the hook. Waiting for his instructions, she sat beside him beneath an old pine tree, its sap oozing from the trunk. Shuddering at the image of the worm, Jackie's voice boomed over the line returning her to the present.

"Hello. Sandy is that you? For heaven's sake where are you? We've been worried sick." Jackie sounded upset and rather angry.

"I'm sorry. I couldn't help being so late. My car died and, oh, there's too much to tell over the phone. I'll explain when I get there. I'm in Laramie now."

"Well, how did you get to Laramie if your car broke down and what can't you tell me over the phone?" Jackie sounded disgusted rather than worried. "Friday's Grandpa's funeral, you know."

"Yes, I know." Sandy sighed. "It's a long story. Can someone there come get me?" She leaned on the desk in the small office as she listened to Jackie and stroked the replica of the jackalope sitting beside her. She smiled at the mounted jack rabbit with antelope horns. Grandpa had taken two Englishmen hunting for the illusive animal. A lump climbed to her throat as she remembered that Englishmen came to the ranch before. Were they searching for the brooch then?

"Yes," she heard Jackie reply. "Where are you?"

Sandy described the small market then, as she replaced the receiver, she saw Dusty rush into the office, an anxious expression on his face.

"Our friends are here," he said. "I think they saw me standing outside. They sure don't act like family. Or maybe they do. He peered back into the store then closed the office door. "Anyway, they're out there." His gaze darted around the room and stopped at a window behind the desk. "No back door. We'll have to use the window."

Sandy opened the door a crack and saw the owner point toward the office. She turned to Dusty franticly fighting to open the window. "They're coming," she whispered as she rushed to his side.

"The thing's stuck," Dusty grumbled as he worked to free their only escape route. "Looks like it's painted shut."

Sandy fought the window with him until she heard Sterling's voice outside the door then looked anxiously at Dusty.

Dusty pointed to the opening under the desk.

Sandy shook her head. "It's not big enough," she whispered then glanced at the door and pulled Dusty behind her toward the turning knob. They stood motionless beside the door, so, hopefully, when it opened, they would be behind it.

"It works in the movies," she said softly.

Dusty rolled his eyes and sighed. "This isn't the movies. It doesn't work in real life."

"Sh," she hushed him as the door opened and Sterling peered into the office.

Sandy's reasoning in moving to the door was to slip out when the man came into the office, but that plan quickly faded as Sterling stood at the open door surveying the room then peeked around the door at the couple hiding there. She gasped when she saw his cruel smile and gritted her teeth, shoved the door as hard as she could sending Sterling to the floor. Quickly the two stepped from behind the door and Sandy kicked the man trying to get to his feet.

Dusty joined in the battle as Sterling grabbed Sandy's foot. With all his strength, Dusty doubled his hand into a fist and hit Sterling's protruding chin. In agony Dusty held his hand as Sandy grabbed his sleeve and pulled him from the room.

Sandy looked back once as they scrambled down the store's isle toward the door leading outside and saw Sterling sitting on the floor shaking his head. As they passed Livingstone, Sandy gave him a shove and he landed among the bags of potato chips. Once out the door she stopped momentarily searching for someplace to hide until the car came from the ranch to pick them up. Across the street she saw a motel and shook her head at its possibilities. Then her gaze moved to the overpass and the tracks of the Union Pacific glistening in the company's floodlights. She pulled Dusty's arm and motioned for him to follow.

A single lane paved road lay between the overpass and the small market providing access to old unkempt residences, an electrical power station and a bottling company beyond the small market. Sandy and Dusty raced down the single lane road and passed the giant concrete pillars that held the overpass above the rails. Gasping for breath, Sandy stopped behind the pillar.

Dusty slipped behind the structure beside her and peered around its edge toward the road. "I don't see them," he said. "Maybe they didn't see us come under here."

"Someone from the ranch is coming to get us," Sandy said pointing to the overpass above them. "We have to get up there, so they'll see us." Her gaze roamed the well-lit rail yard, its floodlights illuminating the tracks and freight cars sitting on the far rails.

"There," Dusty said pointing south of the overpass. "Stairs going up. There must be a walkway up there."

Sandy's gaze darted from the freight cars to the flight of steel steps leading upward. She peeked around the concrete support. "Let's get up there."

They had to retrace their escape path to get to the stairs, and with their attention only on their destination, they looked neither left nor right so consequently they didn't notice Sterling step from behind a concrete support.

Sandy's heart pounded inside the western shirt and her hands trembled as she gazed up the stairs and stepped onto the first flat metal surface.

Dusty, in a quick glance backward, grabbed Sandy around the waist, pulled her from the stairs and escorted her behind the stairs into the yard of an old residence that looked like it stood in its location long before the overpass existed. They hid behind a dilapidated shed that had, long years ago, housed a horse to pull the now wheelless wagon that laid beside the run down structure.

"Now what?" Dusty asked as he peered around the corner of the shed.

Sandy gazed west of the shed to the railroad yard. "Maybe we can get to those freight cars over there. It looks dark enough to hide us."

Dusty looked across the well-lit, open rails and the cars sitting on the far track. "Let's do it then," he said, nodding in agreement.

They raced from the protection of the shed across the gravel and over the first set of rails. The floodlights made the going easy. Sandy chanced a glance behind her and saw Sterling momentarily stop at the shed then start toward the rail yard. In looking backward, she didn't see the second set of tracks and tripped on the silver rail. She landed hard on the ties and sat rubbing her knee and groaning as she felt blood trickling from the wound.

"Don't fret about that," Dusty warned as he pulled her to her feet. "I think our friend intends giving us wounds much more deadly," he said grabbing her around the waist and carrying her across the next set of rails. "We'll have to crawl under the freight car," he said nodding at the train cars in front of them.

They scrambled beneath the freight car and out the other side then stood clinging to each other, gasping for breath, and listening for Sterling's step.

Sandy finally motioned toward the houses beyond the rails; small dwellings with light splashing from their windows.

Dusty nodded in agreement as they raced from the rails to the old part of town. Dogs barked as they fled down dark alleys and people popped their heads out the windows yelling for the animals to be quiet.

The couple stopped in front of a long warehouse spreading the length of the block that barred their escape.

Dusty banged on the building. "They had to put it right here, didn't they?"

Sandy ignored his question, gazing one way then the other along the length of the building. She pointed to the right, down the alley behind the structure. "I hear cars that way. That's probably where the highway runs toward the ranch. Maybe we can still catch that ride." She left Dusty and ran down the alley.

"Hey, wait for me," Dusty said as he took one more look behind him and spied Sterling stepping from behind a house opposite the warehouse. "He's coming. He's behind us," he yelled as he raced after Sandy.

They quickly retraced their steps to the front of the warehouse and crossed the street to a row of houses that ended the old section of town. Before them spread dark open country and far beyond they saw the lights of a newer part of town where residents longed for country living yet reside close to town.

"Looks like a long way over there," Dusty said with a sigh.

"Do we have a choice?" Sandy asked a she gazed behind them at the man hurrying up the street.

"Let's do it," Dusty said and dashed from the lights of town into the darkness of the grasslands.

Sandy stumbled after him over the uneven ground as she tried to keep her attention on the lights beyond and the highway that rose above the west section of town.

Then Dusty stopped still in the darkness. "It's wet," he said raising his foot and shaking water off his boot.

"I forgot," Sandy said straining to look into the darkness. "I forgot about the river. It's overflowing this time of year."

"That's great." Dusty sighed in defeat. "The river in front of us and a madman behind us." He gazed back the way they came, but only darkness met his gaze. "What do you suggest? We're between him and a wet place, here."

Sandy trembled in the darkness. "I don't know." Her voice shook and she stepped close to Dusty. "I don't know."

Chapter 10

The full moon rose behind the Summit. It sent a wave of soft light across the rocks of Vetauwoo, into the shadowy backstreets of Laramie and rippled across the wet bottomlands close to the river.

Sandy and Dusty, wrapped in each other's arms, watched the bright rocky face peek over the buildings far to the east and slowly chase the darkness to the snowy hills to the west. The soft moonlight left an eeriness as it pushed among the grasses and shone on the couple standing in ankle deep water.

Sandy gazed toward the buildings behind her searching for a lone figure. Sterling could no longer cover his presence in a cloak of darkness, nor could she and Dusty. She felt Dusty pulling on the sleeve of her blue jacket and pointing into the moonlit marsh. Her gaze followed the finger's direction to a man, stooping, trying to make himself look small in the soft lightness.

Sandy's face filled with anxiety when she saw him stand. "He's seen us," she whispered.

Dusty motioned toward the willows and chokecherry bushes lining the banks of the river. "Come on," he urged. "Into the bushes. We stick out like toads on a rock." He helped her through the water, deepening as they neared the river.

Sandy cringed as the cold water reached her knees. "I need a bath, but this is ridiculous."

She stepped into the willow bushes beside Dusty and watched him push the branches aside, giving him a clearer view of the wet grassy flatlands between them and the outskirts of town.

"See him?" she whispered as she made an opening for herself.

Dusty shook his head and closed the opening of branches. "He's out there. We just can't see him." He looked behind them at the river. Deep water rushed down its original bed pushing the excess over its banks onto the surrounding lowlands. Dusty sighed with defeat as he watched the water race toward a bridge over which traffic passed. "There's no way we can cross that water," he said, then studied the bridge less than a quarter mile away. "If we could get to the highway, maybe we could catch a ride."

Sandy closed her branched opening and gazed at the river then the highway over it. "Sterling would see us for sure if we made a break for it." She saw him nod in the moonlight.

"We're cornered like a mountain cat," he said, slipping off his Stetson and peering through the branches again.

Sandy lifted her foot, shook the water from it and placed it in the wet coldness again. She wished she had chosen the higher cowboy boots, but then, there'd just be that much more water in them.

An idea zipped through her mind as she watched Dusty peer through the branches. "You know what a mountain cat would do, don't you?"

Dusty quickly turned to face her. "He'd fight. He wouldn't just hide in the bushes." He sobered a minute. "Okay. What does that have to do with us?"

Sandy saw his smile appear and found comfort in it. She smiled back at the beaming eyes and the moonlight that caught in his thick blond hair giving him a halo.

"She'd fight." Sandy emphasized the female gender.

"Yeah." Dusty turned serious again. "But where's our claws?"

Sandy searched around their branchy prison for a weapon. "Don't just stand there," she ordered him. "Look for a big branch or something to hit him with. We have to do something. We just can't wait for him to do whatever he plans to do."

"You're right. You're really right this time." Dusty said as he began searching for a large branch. "I just hope he doesn't have a gun."

"A gun?" Sandy stopped searching as fear flashed through her. "A gun." I didn't think of that You don't suppose he'd have a gun would you?" She watched him select branches from the willow bush then frantically plunged her arms into the water hunting for some kind of weapon. Finally, she pulled a sturdy club from the water, rose slowly, and jammed her fists on her hips. "And what do you mean I'm right this time?" she asked as she pulled a sturdy branch from the river bed.

He chuckled and broke a branch from the willow bush. "Your record of being right really isn't good," he said playfully holding the limp willow switch to protect himself from her raised club.

"I guess you're right," she said lowering her weapon and pointing to the switch he held. "Is that what you'll use against Sterling?"

"Well, what do you suggest? Do you have something from the movies to help us out of this one?" He dropped the switch and searched for something larger.

"Here, you take this," she said handing him her club. Reaching back into the water she pulled out a large stone. "Yes. I'll use something from the Stone Age."

"Okay," he said slowly. "We just step out and I'll club him, and you stone him to death. Is that your plan?"

She huffed disgustedly at him. "He'll be coming. We just watch and when he's close enough, we use our weapons."

A soft chuckle rose in Dusty's throat. "You never say die, do you?"

"Well, what do you suggest? I'm open to suggestions."

Dusty slowly shook his head and gazed at the rushing water behind them then pushed the branches of the willow aside and looked toward the open land. "We'll give it our best shot," he concluded.

She nodded emphatically in agreement. "Do you see him yet?" She held the large stone, ready to throw it.

"Nothing." Dusty closed the opening. "This is getting spooky. Where could he be?"

Sandy shivered as the chill west wind blew from the river. She lowered the stone, blew the air from her lungs, and listened to the silence growing around them.

"He's there," she whispered. "I know he's out there."

Dusty raised his hand for silence. "Listen," he whispered as he pulled the branches aside. "Sounds like someone walking in the water."

Sandy raised the stone, listening for the sloshing Dusty heard and readied herself to throw the weapon. A movement in the moonlight beside Sandy caused her to turn. There stood Sterling holding a gun. She wanted to raise the stone and throw it, but instead she froze to the spot, unable to move. Only her heart drumming inside her chest told her she was still alive.

"Drop the stone, little lady," he said.

Sandy slowly lowered the rock and let it fall into the water. She looked anxiously toward Dusty but saw only the swaying willows left by his quick departure.

"Where's your friend?" Sterling asked, his gaze searching the willows.

Sandy gazed at the empty spot where Dusty had stood. It seemed the willows had swallowed him. She quickly turned back to Sterling, realizing she was alone. "I don't know," she finally said. "He's not with me. He ran to the road instead of coming with me." Hoping he believed her lie, she looked away from the willow grove and directly at her assailant.

"Protecting him, huh?" Sterling smiled and aimed the gun toward the bushes and fired three times.

Sandy cringed as the bullets zinged through the willows. She looked away from Sterling's target fighting the tears filling her eyes. "You didn't have to shoot him," she yelled. "He has nothing to do with this."

Sterling ignored her anger and held out his free hand. "Finally," he said. "The brooch. Give it over."

Fear changed to anger as Sandy watched the man with the gun. "Who are you, anyway? You're not a relative. And what is this about a brooch? I don't know anything about a dumb brooch," she screamed at him.

"No, I'm not a relative," Sterling confessed. "But I overheard the brooch's value as I drove your cousin to the airport."

"You're a chaffier," Sandy said as her eyes widened.

"And a bodyguard," he added.

"And Livingstone?" she asked.

"He's the Templeton's accountant in England. His family has been their money watchers for years. And now we must have the gem your grandfather left to you. It will complete the original collection. Only then will it be worth a fortune." He chuckled. "And that fortune will be mine."

From the corner of her eye, Sandy saw Dusty approaching with the raised club in his hands and she knew she must keep Sterling's attention on her and not on Dusty creeping up behind the gunman. She felt her heart pumping her blood frantically through her brain and her breath came in large gasps. With her eyes directly on Sterling, she took a deep breath and slammed her hands on her hips.

"Well, what does this brooch look like? There are lots of those things in people's jewelry boxes. How do you know what it looks like?" She spoke slowly and loud enough to cover the sloshing of Dusty's boots in the water.

"It matches the set," Sterling said. "And I've seen the eleven gems in the collection. It's a ruby and I'll have it to make an even dozen."

"Then you just as well have it," Sandy yelled. "It's right here in my pocket." She lied as she pushed her hand into the pocket of her Levi's. "Yes, I just as well let you have it." She emphasized the words, let you have it, hoping Dusty would hasten his arrival.

The slosh of Dusty stepping through the water caused Sterling's gaze to quickly move from her, his gun moving with him as if it were part of his arm and as he changed his position, Sandy screamed and grabbed Sterling's arm causing the discharged bullet to zing into the water at Dusty's feet.

Without hesitation Dusty swung the club hitting the arm holding the gun. The weapon fell from Sterling's hand into the water and as Sterling dove for the weapon, Sandy jumped on him landing both of them both in the river. She hung on like a wood tick as he tried to push her off and retrieve the gun.

"Get the gun," she screamed to Dusty, who stood with the club above his head, waiting for an opening to use it.

Dusty dropped the club and groped in the water for the gun. "I can't find it," he said as he crawled on hands and knees in the water.

Finally, Sterling rose in the water and forcefully picked Sandy off him and threw her aside. She felt the water splash around her and fought to keep her head above the wetness. Frantically splashing, she got to her feet and as she stood with water running down her face from the frizzy blond hair, she smiled.

Dusty held the wet gun firmly in his hand pointing it at Sterling. "You okay?" Dusty asked her. He drew his attention to her for only a second, but that gave Sterling enough time to break into a run heading back across the lowlands toward town.

"Stop or I'll shoot," Dusty shouted, but Sterling continued splashing through the wet grass.

As Sandy waded to his side, he lowered the gun. "Well," he said. "It works in the movies."

Sandy took the gun from him and threw it into the river. "I don't want to see that ever again."

"What are you doing? We might need that. Now we're back to sticks and rocks," Dusty told her.

"Then sticks and rocks it is," she said, shaking the water from her sleeves. "Anyway, he doesn't have it."

Dusty shrugged. "Sure, seemed like a good idea to me. Do you think that's the last we'll see of Sterling?" He jammed his fists onto his hips. "Probably not. They're determined to get that brooch."

She flashed a surprised look at him. "Then you heard?"

"Yes," he said. "Do you really have that brooch in your pocket?"

"No." She shook her head. "I've never even seen it even if it does exist. Those fellows must be mistaken."

"They sure are persistent for running after a lost cause," Dusty said. "I really think there must be something to it."

"We'll get this all cleared up when we get to the ranch. My grandmother will know if this illusive brooch exists."

"Well," he sighed. "What's next? How do you presume we get to your grandmother? I suppose we just as well start walking."

She nodded and looked at the tall, blond man standing beside her waiting to hear her next move. Something stirred inside her as she saw the clear blue eyes grow warm with feeling for her. She swallowed a lump rising in her throat. "I'm glad Sterling didn't shoot you. I was afraid he'd got you for sure."

Dusty wiped the water running down his face. "He didn't even come close," he said softly. His arm moved across her shoulder, and she welcomed it as she stepped closer to him.

She stood for a long moment in the comfort of his embrace. "Well," she sighed and stepped away from him. "We'd better get out of here. "We can probably catch a ride when we get to the highway."

They waded until the ground became higher enabling them to run. Sandy stopped only once to lean on Dusty and pour the water from her boots.

Dusty chuckled as he emptied his own boots. "Now we know how a frog feels," he said.

She giggled and stepped to the edge of the highway. "Then we'd better hop to it," she said over her shoulder.

Dusty nodded and shook his head at her bad joke then followed her across the highway where they hoped to catch a ride with someone going west.

As they walked along the edge of the road, a pickup, packed with singing young people, stopped, the rock music filling the air.

"You guys fall in the river?" the young man asked from the open window on the passenger side.

"Sure did," Dusty said, urging forth his western drawl. "How far you goin'?"

"Just out here to this café. Want a lift?"

Sandy pulled on Dusty's shirt. "I can call the ranch from there."

Dusty nodded to the young man tipping the can of beer to his lips. "Yeah," Dusty said. "You can drop us there."

"Climb in the back, there." The young man motioned toward the pickup bed.

Sandy and Dusty climbed into the open pickup bed close to the cab and hung on as the driver jerked forward. They huddled close together as the chill wind blew their wet clothes.

As the pickup crossed the river bridge, Sandy pointed at the car following. "That wouldn't be them would it?"

Dusty pulled her toward him and lay down in the pickup box. "Could it be anyone else?"

Chapter 11

Dusty peered over the pickup box and watched Livingstone pass by the truck and speed ahead of them. "Looks like he found Sterling," he said as he sat back down beside Sandy. "But I don't think they know we're here."

Sandy cuddled close to him, trying to draw some of his body heat through her wet clothes. "Thank goodness. I've had about all of Sterling I can stand." She hugged herself as the cool night air surged around the cab and she welcomed Dusty's arm over her shoulders.

The pickup stopped at a traffic light that enabled autos coming off the interstate easier access to the state highway. Further on, the road forked south to Colorado and west to the snowy mountains and the ranch.

Sandy shivered in the chill, longing for the café's warmth and a hot cup of tea. As the pickup proceeded, she saw Sterling and Livingstone pass them again. "There they are again," she told Dusty. "But I think we'll be safe at the café even if they cruse the road all night. They won't know where we are." She sighed with relief. "I'll call Jackie again and she'll come. That should be the end of them. They must not know where the ranch is, or they'd already be there." She felt herself rambling but couldn't seem to stop.

Dusty's arm tightened around her shoulder. "It's alright," he said. "It will be alright."

The restaurant's lights streamed into the darkness as Sandy and Dusty climbed stiffly from the pickup box. Beside the eating place stood a motel complex and Sandy thought how welcome a warm bed would be but shook her head at the thought as she saw a pay telephone in the entryway. Shivering, she dialed and waited for Jackie to pick up the phone. She wiped at her wet jacket then heard Jackie's irritated voice.

"What in the world is going on?" Jackie asked. "You weren't where you said you'd be."

"I know," Sandy sighed. "We have these two guys chasing us."

"Chasing you?" Why? Have you done something? Now, come on, Sandy, tell me what's going on."

"They want a brooch they think I have that belonged to our great grandfather or maybe a greater one. Do you know of such a thing?"

"No," Jackie said slowly. "I've never heard of a brooch."

"I thought I'd ask Grandma. Maybe she'd know." Sandy stood on one foot then the other trying to warm her feet. "Anyway, we're at this café and motel west of town. Do you know where I mean?"

"Oh, yes," Jackie answered. "But who do you mean by we? Is someone with you?"

"Yes, he's helped me a lot," Sandy nodded to the phone.

"He?" Jackie asked.

"Yes, he's a man." Sandy became aggravated with the questioning. "I'll tell you about it when you get here."

"Okay. It will be a while. There's a lot going on here. Lots of people to bed down and feed. They've come for the funeral, you know."

"We'll get something to eat here," Sandy told her. "And we'll be waiting. Just please come as soon as you can." She replaced the receiver and walked to an empty booth.

"What's the new plan?" Dusty asked as he stepped beside her.

"She's coming to pick us up here," Sandy said as they sat down in a booth. "I just hope we can get together this time."

"How about a burger? That sound good to you?" Dusty asked as he studied the menu.

"Doesn't anything upset you?" she asked, annoyed at his disinterest in their situation.

"Sure. Nothing I can do about it. Sterling and the accountant are running up and down the road out there and all we have to do is wait and hope your sister gets here before those other two figure out where we are." He ordered two hamburgers and hot tea. "Just have to keep it all in perspective."

"In perspective? It is all so warped it'll never be the same." She stirred sugar into her tea. "Of course, it doesn't really involve you."

"No, course not. I can't get involved just because someone wants to kill me." Dusty said as the waitress served the meal and he layered his hamburger with catsup.

"Are they really still out there?" She looked at her sandwich and nibbled on the fries.

"Oh, yes. Driving up and down the road." His gaze flashed to the door. "I almost expect them to come walking in any minute."

"They didn't see us in that pickup. I know they didn't." She lifted the burger's bun and gazed at the meat inside. "How could they?" She covered the meat with mustard and replaced the bun.

"I don't know." Dusty bit into the burger and washed it down with the tea. "When should your sister be here?"

Sandy looked at the clock above the cash register and gasped. "Is it really almost two in the morning? Jackie said it would be a little while. There are a lot of people at the ranch."

They finished the meal and sipped on the tea, their gaze on the door, watching for Jackie and hoping Sterling wouldn't step through.

"Well, what do you think? Should we think of a place to spend the night?" Dusty asked as he paid for the meal. "We might be stuck here until morning. Well, later this morning," he said motioning at the clock.

Sandy turned her back on his smiling face and stepped into the entryway. "Jackie will be here," she protested. "We just have to wait."

"You know what happens when we wait. Those two fellows catch up with us," Dusty said as he stepped outside.

"Well, we can't keep moving. Jackie will never find us," Sandy said as she trotted beside him.

"Well, how about a hot bath and some sleep?" he waved his arm toward the motel.

Sandy felt a sudden chill but shook it off. A hot bath would feel so good. And a bed. It seemed months since she slept in a bed, but all her pleasurable thoughts fled when she saw a long dark car pull up and Sterling and Livingstone bound out leaving the car's motor running in their haste to catch the couple.

Chapter 12

The early morning sun penetrated the coolness that existed at Laramie's seven thousand feet and left chill shadows behind the buildings on Main Street. It warmed the Laramie River and its overflow and the motel and restaurant where Sandy and Dusty stood momentarily staring at Sterling and Livingstone clambering from their auto, its motor running, ready for the abduction.

Sandy bounded, planning to follow Dusty, who ran toward the motel, but Sterling caught her by the arm and carried her, kicking, and screaming, toward the car.

"Put me down, you bumbling idiot. Put me down." Sandy yelled as her boots banged against his legs.

Sterling growled at her and stumbled over her battering feet sending both of them onto the paved parking lot. The gunman quickly got to his feet, grabbing at Sandy as she squirmed away on her hands and knees.

Sterling stopped his groping for her when Dusty ran at him from behind and pulled him from his quarry by the collar of his jacket. Sterling rose and ferociously dove at Dusty sending him to the pavement with a blow to his stomach. Then he turned to Sandy.

Sandy gazed at Sterling disgustedly as she watched Dusty get to his feet. As Sterling grabbed for her, she kicked him and began hitting him with her fists.

Dusty jumped him from behind and Sterling tried to fight off both attackers.

"Livingstone," he yelled. "Come and help."

The shorter, older Livingstone reluctantly left the safety of his observation point beside the car and grabbed Dusty's arm, but the younger man yanked himself free and jumped back at Sterling. Livingstone pulled Dusty from his partner and ducked Dusty's flying fists.

Sandy squealed as Sterling grabbed her, pinning her arms to her sides and, once again, started toward the car.

Dusty's fist landed hard in Livingstone's stomach, then he grunted in satisfaction, and raced to Sandy's aid, grabbing Sterling's sleeve he loosened the hold around Sandy.

Sandy ran, not knowing or caring which direction she took. Puffing, she glanced over her shoulder and saw Sterling racing after her and Dusty getting to his feet to follow.

Sterling grabbed her and held her tight forcing her back toward the car. She saw Dusty fighting off Livingstone and sent the heel of her boot into Sterling's shinbone forcing him to limp, but his hold on her remained secure. She battered him with her elbows only to have him hold her tighter and as he forced her toward the car's open door, Dusty appeared and landed solid blows to Sterling forcing him through the open door and into the back seat. As Livingstone arrived to assist, Dusty sent him to the ground and grabbed Sandy's hand.

"Let's get out of here," he said, pulling her behind him.

Sandy saw Livingstone raise and Sterling crawl from the back seat then continue their pursuit.

Dusty pulled her around the corner of the restaurant, and she leaned against the back wall of the café trying to catch her breath. "I hope Jackie doesn't come," she said. "I'd hate to get her into this mess. No telling what these madmen will do."

"At the moment, the madder of the groups has the upper hand," he said as he gazed down the restaurant's wall. "We're chickens ready to be plucked standing here."

Sandy quickly looked toward one corner of the building then the other. The back door of the kitchen caught her attention, standing ajar and letting the morning's coolness into the cooking area. She pointed to the door then pulled Dusty after her.

"Come on, in here. Maybe we can disappear for a while, anyway," she said.

They slipped through the kitchen door and closed it. The kitchen help looked at them momentarily as they hurried through their tasks.

Dusty pushed his Stetson to the back of his head and smiled. "Just go about your work. We're just here to inspect for cleanliness." He ran his hand across a counter lined with plates. "This could stand a little more."

Sandy giggled, grabbed his arm, and pulled him into the eating area. "What are you doing? They know we aren't inspectors."

Dusty shrugged. "How would they know? I look inspectorish."

She grinned at his soiled Levi's and matching jacket and the broad brimmed hat atop the thick blond hair. "You look like anything but an inspector for cleanliness."

"Humm," he mused. "I washed my hands last night, I think." He chuckled deep in his throat then gazed out the restaurant windows motioning at the two men standing outside. "Do you suppose they're gathering forces?"

Sandy sat in a booth where she could watch the window. "It looks like it." Her eyes grew wide as she saw them coming toward the glass door. "They're coming in," she said as she slipped from the booth.

As they rushed into the kitchen Dusty tipped his hat and smiled nervously. "Everything checks out," he told the kitchen workers. "Everything's spick and span," he said as he yanked on the door and held it open for Sandy.

"We have to find a hiding place," she said as she gazed around the grounds. "There," she said pointing to the trucks in the parking lot, "Behind that big truck."

They raced to the truck and stopped behind the large vehicle. Sandy peered around the high fender and saw Sterling step from the kitchen door watching him look one way then the other, his keen eyes catching every movement. Livingstone joined him outside the kitchen door as Sterling motioned for them to search in different directions.

Sandy moved back behind the truck, hiding behind the large tires. "They're searching behind the café," she whispered. "We can't stay here." She looked beyond the truck to the open land stretching before her. "There doesn't look like any place to hide out there." Slumping against the tire, she sighed. "What a mess. We can't run and we can't stay."

Dusty removed the Stetson and peeked around the truck's grill then quickly pulled back. "Sterling's coming around the back of the truck," he whispered. "We'll have to do something."

Sandy gazed toward the end of the truck's trailer then at the motel complex in the opposite direction. "Come on," she said. "Let's try and make it behind the motel." She darted from behind the truck and began running, her attention on the motel that seemed far away. She chanced a glance over her shoulder and saw Dusty racing after her and beyond, Sterling watched them.

The two men urged her to run faster. She darted behind the motel and raced along the horseshoe shaped structure, turning the corner, and looking down the long unbroken wall. On she raced pausing only long enough to test the locked back doors of the building. She stopped at the end of the wall and looked back.

"Don't stop now," Dusty panted as he stopped beside her. "Get around the corner."

Sandy fought for breath as she watched the man racing behind her. One man. Her eyes grew large. Livingstone was behind them. Where was Sterling?

Dusty grabbed her hand and jerked her around the corner then pulled her along the shorter wall, which led to the parking lot.

"Sterling," she puffed. "Sterling's not behind us."

Dusty slowed his pace as he neared the corner. He stopped before stepping into the parking lot and peered around the corner at Sterling gazing from one end of the building to the other. "Sterling's waiting for us," Dusty said dryly.

Sandy stepped to the corner and peeked around it. She saw Sterling pacing back and forth in front of the motel.

The man behind them hurried the couple's decision and Sandy stepped from cover running toward the parked cars in front of the café. She saw Sterling spy them and she and Dusty kept the cars between them and the gunman. She watched Sterling wait patiently until Livingstone stood beside him then the two moved around the parked cars toward them.

"Do we give up or start the circle again?" Dusty asked, backing away from the pursuers.

"We have to get to the ranch without them," Sandy said, moving with Dusty.

"Any suggestions?" he asked as the car behind them barred their way.

"Run like a wild man," she said and rushed toward Sterling giving him a mighty shove and knocking him aside.

Dusty finished sending Sterling to the pavement as he passed by and followed Sandy toward the road.

Sandy stopped at the road and looked back at the two men approaching. Her gaze darted from the pursuers to the cars passing by them then back to the parking lot frantically searching for a secure place to disappear from view. Then she saw it. Sterling's large dark car, its doors open and the engine running. A smile pulled at the corners of her mouth as she grabbed Dusty's sleeve. "Come on," she said as she raced to the car. She gazed at the two men changing direction to follow them as she slipped behind the steering wheel.

"Why didn't we think of this a long time ago?" Dusty asked as he slid in the passenger seat and slammed the door.

"Too busy just running," she said and jammed the automatic into drive and stomped on the foot feed. The tires squealed as the powerful motor forced the car forward. As she pulled onto the road, she glanced back at the parking lot and saw the two men shaking their fists and screaming something she'd rather not hear.

She laughed out loud as she steered the car west leaving Sterling and Livingstone far behind. Sighing deeply, she pushed the foot feed and the car surged forward. "Almost home," she told Dusty.

"I can go for that," he said, leaning his head on the seat. "I wonder if your sister came to get us."

"I don't know. Right now, I want to get far away from those two men."

"They'll probably find out where your ranch is," Dusty reminded her.

"Yes, I suppose. Jackie said there are lots of people out there staying overnight. We have to warn them about Sterling and Livingstone."

"Overnight is over," Dusty said, gazing out the window. "It's Thursday already."

"Tomorrow's the funeral and we have to get a little sleep and talk to Grandma." She swallowed a lump in her throat and wiped tears forming in her eyes. "I wish Grandpa were there. He'd know all there is to know about owning a brooch."

"How about your mother? Would she know?"

Sandy shook her head. "She died some years ago. It's just been Dad, Grandpa, Grandma, and Jackie and me."

"Oh," Dusty said. "I'm sorry."

"That's alright. I've had a happy life. Well, until now, that is. I could have done without this part."

"Oh, I don't know," Dusty smiled. "We wouldn't have met without this part."

Sandy smiled and nodded. "That part of this catastrophe is quite nice."

"Hey, what's that big ditch on our left, over there?" Dusty craned his neck to see the large depression in the ground. "It looks like it goes on for miles."

"It's the Big Holler," Sandy said. "It's pretty long. I don't remember how it was formed. During the ice age or something, but it runs clear to the town at the foot of those snowy mountains. The ranch is down there."

Dusty gazed at the depression in the earth. Its edges looked as though they had been smoothed by a giant roller and at the bottom of the scooped out hollow cattle grazed peacefully on its grasses.

Sandy turned to the left off the road then gasped as she looked at the gas gage. "This hog is about out of gas."

"That's not all," Dusty said gazing down the road. "It looks like Sterling and Livingston found a car. They're on our trail."

Sandy stepped on the gas petal and the big car coughed and wheezed then stopped dead still. She looked behind then at the approaching car.

"Any more suggestions?" Dusty asked.

Chapter 13

Sandy turned the key in the ignition repeatedly and leaned forward encouraging the car to move. She stomped on the foot feed to squeeze a little more gas into the engine and angrily beat her fists on the steering wheel.

As they sat at the bottom of the Big Holler thunderheads began to build over the snowy mountains. Their dark flat bottoms hovered close to the earth and rumbled inside as though angry at the land below.

Sandy looked at the clouds. "Rain," she grumbled. "That's all we need." She slapped at the steering wheel. "We're not far from the ranch." She pointed out the windshield. "See, over there? You can see the house from here."

Dusty looked toward the west at the buildings in the distance. "What is it half a mile, maybe?"

"Not much more. Shall we make a run for it?" She said as she opened the door.

"No," Dusty said, stopping her. "They'll just run us down with the car. We need a plan."

Sandy closed the door and pushed the lock down. "I can't think of anything but running." She gazed out the windshield at the ranch so close, yet so far away.

Dusty glanced out the back window. "Here they come." He leaned toward Sandy. "Okay, here's a plan. We have to make sure they're both out of the car. Then I'll keep them occupied while you run to the ranch."

Sandy shook her head. "But what about you? You can't fight both of them off." She shook her head again. "No, I can't let you do that."

Dusty sighed deeply as car doors slammed behind them. "I don't see any other way."

Sandy slumped in the seat then looked out the back window and her eyes widened as she saw the man approaching. "Dad," she squealed. "It's my dad and Jackie." She swung the door open and raced into his arms.

"What in the world have you been through?" her father asked as he and Jackie hugged her.

"I'll tell you all about it when we get home, but first I'd like you to meet Dusty. He helped me through all this." She turned to Dusty and smiled. "Dusty, this is my dad, Bradly Templeton and my sister, Jackie Richards. Jackie is married and has two kids."

Dusty stepped forward and shook Bradly's hand. "Glad to finally meet you." He nodded to Jackie. "And you, too."

Jackie didn't wait to shake his hand but wrapped her arms around him. "Thank you so much for helping my sister." She wiped at tears slipping down her cheeks then backed away from him smoothing her long dark hair.

"Well, let's not stand out here," Bradly said, adjusting the Stetson on his own thick dark hair. "Get in the car and let's get you kids home."

Home sounded so good to Sandy. Her heart pounded differently than it did just a few minutes before. Now excitement and relief at being home sent it drumming against her ribs. She fought to keep her eyes open as she heard Jackie and her father talking from the front seat. Their voices began to sound fuzzy, and she was unable to tell one from the other, let alone understand what they were saying. She hoped her input was not requested. Her head flopped against the back seat, and she pulled at her eyelids as the car passed beneath the sign reading Templeton. Everything was the same as the last time she was home. The pastures were as spring green as the lawn circling the two story house.

Beyond, a barn and sheds stood on the greenness and further to the west, Jackie's home sat secluded in a stand of cottonwood trees. She and her husband, Tom, decided not to live in the same house as Bradly, but since the death of Sandy's mother, Jackie and Tom spent a lot of time in Bradly's two story house.

Sandy's brain saw the familiar surroundings rather than her eyes and she felt she was floating upstairs to her bedroom when actually her father was carrying her and laying her on her bed. The storm clouds moved to the east and now dust particles riding on beams of sunlight streamed in the window until Grandmother pulled the curtain closed.

"Grandma Lily," Sandy said. "I have to talk to you." Her voice sounded far away as if it belonged to someone else.

"You just lie there and rest. Talking will come later," Grandma Lily told her.

"I sure could use a bath," Sandy whispered. "I should really take a bath before I sleep." She thought she rose from the bed and went into the bathroom, right off her bedroom, and could almost hear the water running then she heard nothing as the soft blanket of sleep covered her and she welcomed the darkness as her eyes closed.

Restlessness poured through her dreams as she turned from one side to the other evading her captors in her sleep. Waking with a scream, she sat up trying to catch her breath and wiped the sweat from her face. Slowly she began to recognize her surroundings and laid her head on the pillow gazing around the room. She was home and she was safe. The wall paper with tiny rose buds hugging the walls made her smile. Her mother picked it out when Sandy was very young, and Sandy never wanted it changed. The closet opposite the bed still held clothes she'd left here when she acquired the teaching position in Colorado and the dresser stood it its rightful place beside the closet with her mother's picture smiling at her from its frame. She smoothed her blond hair mirrored in the photo, sighed as she nestled beneath the covers then gazed at the shaded window.

"What time is it?" she shouted as she bounded from the bed, flung open the curtains and saw the sun high in the sky. "Oh, boy," she breathed. "Today's the funeral and I don't even know what time it is."

Quickly she drew a bath and slipped into its caressing warmth. This would have to take longer than it should for she didn't want to rush the pleasure the steaming water brought her. The hair washing took less time as all she had to do was towel dry the ringlets the permanent left.

With her hands on her hips, she studied the clothes in the closet then gazed at each article with care. Drawing out a black skirt and white frilly blouse, she nodded, laid them on the bed and checked the dresser. Everything she needed was folded neatly and she picked out underwear and pantyhose. The black flats on the closet floor suited her and she dressed quickly then smoothed the covers on the bed. Taking one last look in the mirror, she stepped out the door and down the wooden stairs sliding her hand along the cherry banister.

She heard the crowd before she saw them and smiled as she stopped at the living room. People were sitting and standing with a cup of coffee in one hand and Grandma Lily's coffee cake in the other. They weren't strangers, but ranchers she knew from childhood. They welcomed her like a lost lamb coming back to the fold.

Her gaze darted from one to another as she searched for one face among the group. Where was Dusty? Had he found a way back to Colorado? She greeted her friends as she passed by then saw him talking to her father and slipped to his side.

"Dusty, here, has been telling me about his cowboy experience in Colorado. I might just have to hire him on," Bradly said.

"Are you alright, Dusty?" Sandy asked him.

"Oh, yes. A good sleep, bath and a hearty breakfast worked wonders," Dusty said.

"I called the ranch where he works," Bradly said. "And told them he'd had an emergency. We'll get him back whenever he wants."

Sandy felt flushed and nodded. "I hope it's not too soon."

"Well, we'll have to see what exciting event happens next," Dusty said, winking at her.

"I hope no excitement at all," Sandy said, shivering at the thought. "I haven't seen Grandma Lily. I really need to talk to her."

"Oh, she's already gone to the gravesite with Jackie and Tom. We'd better get ourselves out there, too." Bradly said as he turned to the group. "It's time we were going now. If you'll follow me."

Sandy grabbed Dusty's hand and followed Bradly to the car. She stopped short seeing Sterling's dark Cadillac.

"It's okay, Sandy," her father said. "I put gas in it and drove it up to the house. It was blocking the road down there."

Sandy nodded and climbed into the back seat of Bradly's Oldsmobile beside Dusty.

"Where's your grandfather going to be buried?" Dusty asked.

"We have our own cemetery a mile or so from here," Sandy said. "It's been in the family for years."

"Sounds good," Dusty said. "We don't want to go to town, I don't think."

"Yes, that *is* good," Sandy said. "I wonder where those guys are."

"Your dad said the police are looking for them," Dusty said.

"I hope they've already found them," Sandy said then pointed out the window. "Here's our cemetery."

As the car stopped, Sandy got out and walked with Dusty, Bradly and the group of friends passed grave stones of those who died in years past then stopped at an open grave and the casket above it. They gathered around Grandma Lily as her pastor read from the Bible.

Sandy tried to listen to the words, but memories blocked the words flowing from the man. She lived with her grandfather since childhood and the thought of no more memories flooded her consciousness. She squeezed Dusty's hand and he held hers tightly.

When the last words were said and the family stood alone watching the casket descend into the ground, Sandy hugged Grandma Lily and clung to her.

"There's one more thing to do," Grandma Lily said. "And we have to do it at the house." She grabbed Sandy's hand. "You and your young man ride home with me."

Sandy followed Grandma Lily to Jackie's car and slipped into the back seat between her and Dusty. "I've been wanting to talk to you," Sandy said.

"When we get to the house," Grandma Lily said. "We'll talk then."

Sandy nodded and leaned against the seat in silence as Tom drove the sad procession home.

Chapter 14

The living room seemed to echo now that all the guests were at Jackie's eating chicken and roast beef. Sandy sighed as she regarded the familiar room. Two overstuffed and leather chairs with foot rests sat against the far wall facing the television with small coffee tables placed beside them. A large leather sofa occupied the wall beneath a picture window facing the west and, today, empty dining room chairs were positioned about the room for the guests who occupied them earlier.

But Sandy's favorite section of the room was the stone fireplace with its chimney rising on the wall where the stairway led to her room. Grandma Lily's love seat sat near the fireplace with her knitting basket on the floor next to where she sat and today, she headed directly for her place by the fire.

"Come on now, Sandy." She patted the cushion beside her. "Sit down and let's talk."

Sandy took a deep breath as Bradly and Dusty each pulled a dining room chair close to the loveseat. "Those two men chasing us were certain I had a brooch that they wanted terribly bad." She studied Lily's wrinkled face. "Does a brooch they're looking for exist at all?"

"Let me tell you the story." Lily folded her hands in her lap. "Many years ago, your great, great grandfather came from England to buy land and develop a cattle ranch. When he left England, he was given money and a piece of jewelry." She cleared her throat. "In case he didn't have enough money to carry him over the years he'd have to live here, he could sell the brooch." She crossed her bony legs one over the other and clasped her hands. "Well, he was very resourceful and made the ranch work." She stretched her arm in front of her. "It was this ranch that he built."

"Then what happened to the brooch? Did he have to sell it?" Sandy asked.

"Oh, no. He kept it to hand down to his children."

Sandy gazed at her father. "Then you have the brooch."

"No, no," Bradly said. "I didn't want anything to do with the thing. I was to give it to your mother, but after she died, I had no use for it."

Sandy turned her attention back to Grandma Lily. "Then you have the brooch."

"Well, your grandfather had it." Lily stopped to take a breath.

"Did he get rid of it?" Sandy asked. "Those men seemed to think I had it."

"Your grandfather received a letter from England sometime in February, I think it was." Lily put her finger to her lips. "Yes, February, I think." She shook her head at Bradly. "Son, go into your father's office. I think that letter is still in the top drawer." Then to Sandy. "It may explain things." She nodded. "Then again, it was pretty vague, to me anyway." Emphasizing with her hands, she continued. "The essence of it was, the relatives in England want to buy the brooch and put it with some others to complete a set. Then they want to put the set in some museum."

Bradly handed the letter to Sandy and read it silently, then nodded. "Okay. Now I get it. Sterling and Livingstone want the brooch before the set is complete. Once the gems are together, they will be out of their reach."

"That's why Sterling is so persistent. Actually, your brooch is the most important one," Dusty said.

Sandy read the letter again, nodding as events began to make sense. "Is this the first letter Grandpa got? It sounds like this is a reply. See here? Is says, beings the brooch will be in your granddaughter, Sandy Templeton's, possession, we will be contacting her. It even has my address in Colorado." She pushed air from her lungs in a huff. "That's how Sterling knew how to find me, and he thought I had the brooch." She gazed at Lily. "Why didn't someone let me know this was going on?"

"Your grandfather was waiting for your visit when your school was out for the summer." Lily shook her head. "We had no idea you'd be going through this terrible experience, or he'd told you what was going on." She shook her head again. "We had no inkling at all."

"Did you know about this letter, Dad?" she asked Bradly.

"Yes. Your grandma, grandpa, and me. We were waiting for you to return home to surprise you with the brooch," Bradly said. "What a surprise we all got."

Sandy shook her head. "I don't understand why giving the brooch to me would be a good thing. The English relatives are the ones who want it."

"Yes," Bradly said. "But if it's in your name, you'll get the reward." He smiled. "You can have a few things you want like going to Europe and places over there you used to talk about."

"All kids talk about being somewhere else. After being in Colorado a couple terms, home looks pretty good," Sandy said as she visually absorbed the room.

"Well, anyway, your grandpa thought he was doing the right thing," Bradly concluded.

"What about Jackie? Why didn't he give the brooch to her?" Sandy asked Grandma Lily. "She could use this reward you're talking about."

"Because he gave it to you," Grandma Lily said.

Bradly rose from his chair and walked to the fireplace. "You were his fishing buddy. You loved going to the cabin with him and doing whatever you two did up there." He gazed at her and sighed. "He just wanted to give it to you, that's all."

Sandy nodded and leaned back against the loveseat's cushion. "Okay then, where is this illusive brooch?"

Lily reached into her sewing basket and pulled out a blue velvet box and handed it to Sandy. "He really wanted you to have this."

Sandy felt her heart thump wildly as she gazed at the box no larger than the palm of her hand. "Is this it? Is this the brooch?"

"Open it and see for yourself," Lily said and smiled mysteriously.

Sandy wondered about the smile and realized something strange was occurring.

"Go on, open it," Dusty said, his eyes flashing with excitement.

Slowly Sandy opened the box and raised her eyebrows at its contents. "Wow. It's the brooch," she said as she ran her fingers over the stone edged with lace of silver. "It's beautiful, but I thought the stone was supposed to be red. This one's blue. I don't understand." She turned to Lily for an explanation.

"Well, I was told a clue is inside," Lily said. "See there? There's a clasp by the stone. You can open it."

"Oh, Grandpa and his tricks. I have to find the real brooch." Sandy said, remembering the fun loving part of the man.

"Go ahead, now," Lily urged. "Pull that little clasp."

"Do you know what's inside?" Sandy asked her.

"I only know some of it, but I do know you're supposed to open it." Lily motioned with her hand. "I'm excited to know what the clue is."

Carefully Sandy pushed the clasp and the stone flipped to the side revealing two pictures, one of Grandma Lily and the other of Grandpa. "I don't understand. Are these pictures Grandpa's clues?" Then she studied the photos closer. "Grandpa's picture has a piece of folded paper stuck in the corner." She pulled the note from the edge of the photo and gazed at Lily. "It is exciting, isn't it? This probably tells me where the next clue is. That's how Grandpa did things." As she laid the brooch in her lap and carefully unfolded the paper, a puzzled expression spread across her face.

"Well, what does it say?" Dusty asked, leaning forward in his chair.

"It says Sapplehead," Sandy said. "Just Sapplehead."

"What in the world is Sapplehead?" Dusty asked. "What kind of clue is that?"

Sandy laughed as she remembered a day long ago. "It's a good clue. A kind of secret, family clue." She leaned back on the loveseat and stared at the ceiling. "You see, when I was about four years old, Grandpa took me fishing at his cabin in the woods by Centennial. He sat under a Ponderosa pine, leaned against the tree, and let his fishing line drift with the current. Suddenly he caught a fish and jerked on the pole, but when he tried to stand, his hair was stuck in the tree's pitch sap. It thought it was very funny and I called him Sapplehead. From then on the cabin site was called Sapplehead."

"Okay," Dusty said. "So, if you want the brooch, you have to go to this cabin."

"Whether she wants to or not, she has to go to Sapplehead," Bradly said. "The quest is in the hunting, not the finding."

"Then it might not even be there," Dusty argued.

"Oh, it's there, alright, but where it is up there is anybody's guess." Bradly shook his head. "This is a difficult game your grandfather thought up."

"I'll bet Sandy knows how to find out. Don't you, Dear?" Lily smiled at her and cocked her head to one side.

Sandy lowered her eyebrows, studying Lily. "I do?" she asked.

"Just think about it for a while," Lily said and rose from her seat. "Now we'd better get up to Jackie's house or those folks will have all the food eaten."

Chapter 15

The guests had departed when Sandy, Dusty, Grandma Lily and Bradly arrived at Jackie's one story ranch house that stretched in all directions to accommodate her growing family. Sandy knew it had two new additions and Jackie appeared to be requiring another nursery.

The dining room table was still laden with food and Sandy took a plate and place chicken, lettuce salad and one of Jackie's fancy vegetable casseroles that Sandy was never quite sure it actually contained. Even the leftovers tasted good, and she decided on a big piece of chocolate cake for dessert, but as she placed it on her plate, she noticed Jackie motioning for her to come into the kitchen situated off the dining room. Jackie's house was modern and had the most update facilities, but Sandy thought she liked Grandma Lily's house better. She sat at the small kitchen table with her piece of cake.

"What is it?" she asked Jackie. "You look worried. Is something wrong?"

Jackie dropped into a chair beside her. "I received a phone call while you were at Dad's place," she said quickly, her breath coming in small gasps.

"Well, what was it about?" Sandy pushed her cake aside and leaned forward.

"I don't know. I said who I was, but he, it was a man, asked to speak to you."

"To me?" Sandy asked. "I wonder why he called here." She stared across the room, not wanting to think who the man might be. "What did he say?"

"He just asked for you and hung up. It was kind of scary."

"You don't suppose it was the police telling me they'd caught those Englishmen." Sandy nodded. "Yes, that's all it probably was." She studied Jackie's worried expression. "Don't you think so?"

"He had an English accent," Jackie said, her voice shaking. "Do you suppose it was one of those men who were chasing you?"

Sandy patted her chest, hoping to restrain her heart from surging to her throat. "If it is, that means the police haven't caught them." She rushed to the phone hanging on the kitchen wall. "I'm calling the police and telling them what's happened. I think they should send someone out to look around."

"You don't suppose they're out here?" Jackie's voice climbed to a higher octave.

"I don't know, but I'm going to find out," Sandy said as she dialed then introduced herself over the phone. Explaining the situation, the man on the other end of the line sounded positive.

"Well, please send someone out here to look around. We have a feeling they may be close by." She replaced the receiver and gazed at Jackie's frightened expression. "They'll send someone as soon as possible." Sandy said.

"What if they're here somewhere? I have kids that play around the out buildings," Jackie said, wringing her hands.

Sandy put her arm around her sister's shoulders. "They're probably not out here at all," she reassured Jackie. "I'm sure the police would call from town if they thought those men would be coming out here."

Actually, Sandy wasn't sure of anything except to inform Dusty and her father of the new events. She found them in the specious living room drinking coffee and laughing at something or other Tom was saying.

As she explained the situation, Dusty and Bradly left their coffee and headed for the door.

"Where are you going?" Sandy asked. "These are dangerous men."

"We'll just scout around," Tom said as he unlocked his gun cabinet beneath a flight of stairs leading to a loft. "Come and take your pick," he told Dusty and Bradly. "Come on, let's end this right here."

Sandy caught Dusty staring at the revolver he chose. "Do you know how to use that?" She wanted to grab his arm impeding his departure, but he only smiled.

"Remember our experience at the river? Yeah, I can use it alright," Dusty told her.

"Be careful. Those guys are desperate. They'll do anything." She wanted to tell them not to go, but she knew they'd do it anyway because they had homes and families to protect. She smiled at their frontier bravery. "Just like the movies," she whispered.

Waiting for the return of the men was more difficult than if she'd grabbed a gun and accompanied them Sandy decided as she paced the living room floor.

"Sit down, now, Sandy," Grandma Lily said. "They're doing all there is to do." She drew needlework from Jackie's sewing basket beside the rocking chair. "Do you want something to do with your hands?"

Sandy rubbed her hands together to wipe the perspiration accumulated there and chuckled. "You know I was never interested in that stuff."

Grandma Lily nodded. "I know, you only wanted to fish and hunt with your grandfather."

"Now I wish I'd taken up the sewing thing." Sandy studied Lily's hands move the needle and yarn as she knitted. "But it would drive me crazy." She plopped into the love seat opposite Lily and gazed out the window facing the sunset. "Maybe they didn't find anything." She nodded at her decision. "There's probably no one out there."

"You're probably right," Lily agreed. "It seems ridiculous for anyone to be hiding out there."

"Yes, it does," Sandy said. She rose from her seat and folded her arms as she returned to her pacing. Stopping at the round table where the men sat, she picked up a cup and saucer then set them down again. The table was not customarily used as a sitting place but was a game center with a board game or cards waiting for players to stop and enjoy themselves, but today the games were put away in the shelves built into the wall beneath the staircase leading to the balcony room that stretched half way across the living room ceiling. Beside the shelves, she hesitated at the glass doors of Tom's gun cabinet and peered at the rifles and pistols. A shiver went through her as she moved from them to the door leading to Jackie and Tom's office where ranch business was conducted. She turned the knob, but the door was locked.

Backtracking, she gazed at the stairway and climbed the wooden steps holding onto the pine banister as she went. She always liked this room, high above the living room. One could hear whatever was going on downstairs yet be alone. She sat on the double bed covered with a blue spread and decorated pillows and welcomed the familiar surroundings. A dresser sat against one wall and paintings by western artists hung on the opposite one. A small window let in the cool June evening and Sandy lay for a moment breathing the freshness wishing all she had to do was recline here not thinking about a thing, but she quickly got to her feet and rushed to the railing at the edge of the loft and gazed at Lily.

"Have they come back yet?" she called to her grandmother.

"No, not yet," came Lily's answer.

As Sandy heaved a sigh and went downstairs, the picture window caught her attention and she stopped, gazing out of the glass at the darkening sky as the first star winked at her. Squinting, toward the barn and out buildings, she tried to capture images of the three men who left the house, but saw only darkness creeping in from the west. Folding her arms again, she returned to Lily.

"Is Jackie still with the boys in their bedroom?" Sandy asked.

"Probably. It takes quite a while to get them washed and bedded down," Lily reminded her.

"Yes, I suppose so. But she's been in there a long time." Sandy gazed into Lily's eyes. "Do you suppose she's alright? If Sterling is around, there's no telling what he'd do."

"I'm sure they're fine," Lily said. "If he is here, our men wouldn't let anything happen."

Sandy gazed toward the dining room. "I think I'll check on them, just to make sure."

"Do as you like," Lily said, studying her needlework. "But I'm sure they're alright."

Sandy stepped into the dining room, gazed out the glass doors leading to the patio, then preceded down the hall where the bedrooms were located. Stopping in the darkened corridor, she listened intently. When she heard nothing, she passed by the master bedroom, the guest chamber and stopped in front of the room where the boys slept. Softly she knocked on the door. "Jackie, are you there?" She turned the knob and peered inside. "Jackie?"

Chapter 16

A nightlight's soft radiance permeated the darkness in the children's bedroom as Sandy entered. She tiptoed in the silence to the two single beds and gazed first at the five year old then the younger boy about three, but Jackie was not in the room. Silently Sandy slipped back into the hall and hearing sounds coming from the bathroom, she hurried to the door.

"Jackie are you in here?" she asked, knocking on the door.

"Yes," Jackie answered. "Come on in."

Sandy stepped into the bathroom, closed the door, and saw Jackie in the tub with bubbles up to her chin.

"I just had to have a bath," Jackie told her. "It looks like you were worried about me," she chuckled into the bubbles.

"Yes, I was," Sandy said as she sat on the lavatory. "When you didn't come back into the living room, I didn't know what to think."

"Did you suppose I was kidnapped or something?" Jackie blew bubbles from her hand.

"Or something," Sandy said. "I just know Sterling won't stop at anything to get rich."

"Oh," Jackie said. "I didn't think of that." She pushed the foam from her chest. "I'd better get out of here and check the doors, anyway the one to the patio. I don't think it's locked."

"I'll check it," Sandy said. "You finish your bath."

Leaving the bathroom, Sandy rushed to the dining room, checked the sliding glass doors and her heart skipped a beat when she found them unlocked. Taking a deep breath, she flipped the outside light switch and scanned the patio. Squinting into the shadows, she studied the cooking area, casting her gaze by the wooden table and matching benches to the grill where Tom cooked steaks and hamburgers then to the lawn chairs in a semi-circle around the barbecue.

"Do you see anything?" Jackie asked, tying her satin robe around her middle as she came into the dining room.

"No," Sandy answered. "Just the men's flashlights. They're coming from the barn, I think."

"I don't really believe they'll find anyone," Jackie said as she began clearing the dining room table.

"I hope not," Sandy said as she carried leftovers to the kitchen and put them in the refrigerator.

"We're pretty far from town, you know, and the police are looking for those guys," Jackie said as she stacked plates in the dish washer.

"You're probably right," Sandy said, wringing out the dish cloth and taking it to the dining room table. "All the same," she said as she wiped the cherry wood. "I think we have to be careful."

"There," Jackie said, wiping her hands on a towel hanging by the sink. "That's done. Now let's go in with Lily and relax."

Sandy followed her to the living room and watched Jackie take needlework from the basket then sit in the love seat opposite Lily, but Sandy couldn't relax and resumed her pacing.

"Will you sit down?" Jackie ordered. "You make me nervous."

"I just can't," Sandy said and walked to the dining room, stared through the patio doors then carefully unlocked them and stepped outside. Surveying the cooking area, she drew in the cool June air and wrapped her arms across her chest. She stopped suddenly as, from the corner of her eye, she saw movement. Was it just a deer or other wild creature? Perhaps she saw only the family dog. Quickly she tiptoed to the shadows behind the table and knelt in the cover of darkness as she watched the form of a man stepping toward the front of the house. She felt her mouth become dry and she licked her lips, but there was nothing to moisten them. The only sound she heard was her heart banging in her ears then quietly and slowly she and moved in the direction the man had taken. Taking a deep breath, she quieted herself and nodded. It's only Dusty or Tom or her father, but possibly the form she observed was none of them. She flattened herself against the wall and peered around the corner surveying the front of the house. A deep sigh and a chuckle escaped from her throat when she saw a police car and Dusty, Tom and her father talking to the uniformed man standing beside the cruiser. Quickly she trotted to them calling, "It's just Sandy. It's just me."

"What are you doing out here?" Bradly asked her.

"Oh, I just stepped out to get some air," she lied. "I saw an officer pass by the patio and knew I was safe."

The expression on the men's faces frightened her and the thumping returned to her chest. "What is it? What's wrong?" she asked.

"He's the only officer here," Dusty said. "And he's been standing right here." He gazed at the policeman. "Were you over by the patio just now?"

Sandy felt a lump crawl to her throat when she saw the officer shake his head.

"Sandy, you go back in the way you came out and lock that glass door," Bradly ordered. "And don't come out here again."

Sandy nodded, turned, and observed the patio with the light she turned on shining brightly into the darkness. Was it Sterling? Had he gone in the unlocked door when she came to the front of the house?

"I'll go back with her," Dusty said.

"And we'll scout around some more," Tom said.

"Come on, Sandy," Dusty said. "Why are you always where you shouldn't be?"

"I'm not," she argued. "I was just curious."

When they reached the patio, Sandy stopped. "We need a plan again."

"Why do we need another one of your plans?" he asked as he clenched his fists on his hips.

"My family is in danger. What if Sterling is here and he takes my family hostage to get the brooch?"

Dusty studied her a moment. "He would do something like that." He shook his head. "He's probably not even here. There's no car. How'd he get here? We know he can't fly."

"I saw someone slip by the patio. I know I did, and it wasn't that policeman." Sandy shook her finger at him.

"Well, it couldn't be Sterling. We'd seen him if he came to the front of the house."

"Maybe he hid when he saw you." Sandy knew she was losing the argument but persisted. "We have to lure Sterling away from the ranch."

"And how do you plan we do that?" Dusty's eyebrows lowered and Sandy knew he was losing patience.

"I know," he suggested. "Why don't you just give him the brooch your grandmother gave you? That should stop all this foolishness."

"Foolishness," she snapped. "You know it isn't silliness." She drew a breath and looked away from him. "Anyway, Sterling knows the gem in the brooch is a ruby. And rubies aren't blue."

"Then what do you propose?" He folded his arms and grunted at her. "How do we lure him away?" He raised his hands above his head. "We don't even know if he's here."

"I think he is. Somehow he got here. Maybe a bird dropped him. I don't know, but I do know we have to make him follow us away from the ranch."

"And where do you propose we lead him?"

"To the place he'll really want to go," she smiled.

"And that is where, back to town?" He crossed his arms and studied her.

"No," she said. "The place where the real brooch is located."

"And where would that be?" Dusty asked, cocking his head.

"Sapplehead," Sandy said and walked into the house.

Chapter 17

Sandy rubbed the chill from her arms, rushed into the living room and saw Jackie working her yarn with the knitting needles. Grandma Lily, still holding her needlework, had fallen asleep with her chin resting on her chest.

"It looks like it's way past time to get Grandma home," Sandy said as she gazed at Lily.

"You can't leave yet. Not until the men are satisfied there's no one out there," Jackie said as she returned her yarn and needles to the sewing basket. "Grandma can stay over and sleep in the guest room."

"Is that what she wants to do?" Sandy asked. "She looks pitiful sitting there like that."

"I'll turn down the covers if you'll wake her," Jackie said as she got to her feet.

"Okay, but you know what she'll say." Sandy said shaking her head.

"I know she'll want her own bed, but you two can't go out there alone." Jackie was persistent. "I'll get the bed ready and be right back."

Sandy gently shook Grandma Lily's shoulder. "Grandma, are you about ready for bed?"

Lily woke with a start. "Oh," she said. "Did I fall asleep?" She yawned and stretched then rose rubbing her back. "Are we ready to go home?"

"Jackie thinks you should stay the night. She's getting the bed ready in the guest room."

"She knows how I feel about that bed. I always wake up with a kink in my neck," Lily said as she rubbed her back again. "Just take me home, Sandy."

"She wants to go home," Sandy said as Jackie came back into the room.

"But I have the bed ready. You just as well stay here. No telling when the men will come back," Jackie pleaded.

"Are they still out there?" Lily asked.

"Yes," Sandy said. "They may be awhile." She saw the yearning in Lily's eyes and sighed. "But if you really want to go, I'll take you."

"I really would like to sleep in my own bed," Lily said.

Sandy gazed at Jackie, who shrugged in defeat.

"Well, whatever you want to do," Jackie said. "But you might as well stay here."

Lily nodded emphatically. "Alright then, Sandy can take me home," she said as she headed for the door.

"Well then, that's settled," Sandy said, trailing after Lily. "Maybe Tom can take Dusty and Dad home."

"Okay, but be careful," Jackie said, following them to the door.

Sandy stepped out behind Lily into the well-lit front yard and helped her grandmother into the car. "All set?" Sandy asked.

"Well, yes," Lily said. "It's been a long day."

"Okay then, home we go," Sandy said as she glanced into the empty back seat and sighed with relief that no one was there. Studying the rear view mirror for a moment and surveying the darkness beyond the yard light, she started the motor, turned on the headlights and shifted into drive. It wasn't far to her father's house, she could walk it in ten or fifteen minutes, but tonight the distance seemed farther, and she urged more speed form the Oldsmobile. As they bumped along over the dirt road, Sandy spied a car's tail lights heading toward the rim of the Big Hollow spewing dust as if its occupants were in a great hurry. Sandy felt a sudden chill and pushed the gas petal.

"We don't need to rush," Lily said, clinging to the seat. "I want to get home in one piece."

"Sorry," Sandy said as she slowed the car and stopped in front of the house. "Guess I was anxious to get home, too." She sat in the car for a moment watching the tail lights of the auto on the road climb to the rim of the hollow and stop. Fear flashed through her, and she felt her blood surging toward her temples. Squinting, she hoped to see the car more clearly, but she knew Sterling's car would be unfamiliar, for his Cadillac sat in her father's driveway and Sterling would have to find another auto.

As she studied the hollow's rim, she noticed Grandma Lily getting out of the car and heading for the house when she stopped. "Are you coming?" Lily asked then her gaze followed Sandy's to the hollow's rim. "What is it? Is that the men chasing you? Maybe it's a policeman waiting for something," she suggested.

"Maybe," Sandy said. "We'd better get inside. You're shivering."

As they entered, Sandy took another look at the car still sitting on the rim then quickly went inside and closed the door. She didn't know if Sterling and Livingstone were in that car, but felt they found her location. It wouldn't be difficult for them to find the ranch, but they would have to secure another car to investigate the back roads of the hollow. Sighing, she brought her attention to Grandma Lily. It had been a long, emotional day for the elderly lady and Sandy observed the exhaustion in her eyes.

"Off to bed with you, Grandma," she said. "I'm going to sit awhile. Dad and Dusty should be back pretty soon."

"There's tea in the kitchen," Lily said as she started to her bedroom beyond the staircase. "Don't stay up too late."

"I won't, Grandma, good night," Sandy said, heading for the large kitchen. Grandma had no dining room, but a long wooden table took up most of the space. Grandma always said she didn't need a dining room but wanted her guests right underfoot. Sandy smiled at the memory and drew a cup of water, put it in the microwave, found a tea bag in the cupboard and sat at the well-worn table.

"A plan," she said "What kind of plan would force Sterling to follow us to Sapplehead?" When she heard the buzzer, she pulled the hot cup from the microwave, dropped the tea bag into it and sat at the table. "Maybe we don't need a plan. Perhaps they're waiting up on the rim, waiting for me to leave the ranch." She pulled the bag from the water and gave it a squeeze. "No, that would probably be too easy." She sipped the tea then reached for the sugar bowl sitting on the table. "Now let's see. They would have to know it was Dusty and me." Scooping a spoon of sugar, she sprinkled it into the tea. "How would they know to follow us to Sapplehead?" She gave the tea a stir and took another sip. "I'll call the police and they could meet us at the cabin." Taking the spoon, she stirred again. "But that would scare them off." Tapping the spoon on the edge of the cup, she studied the ceiling. "It has to be just Dusty and me." She drank from the cup. "Oh, boy. That sounds scary, but what other way is there? Maybe Dusty has an idea." She finished the tea then heard a car in front of the house. Rushing to the door, she saw the police car bringing Dusty and her father home. She hurried outside to the patrolman and pointed to the rim of the hollow. "A car was just sitting up there," she said.

"I'll check it out on my way back to town," the officer said. "Meanwhile, you'd better get inside."

"I think I'll get to bed," Bradly said as they entered. "You two should do the same."

'We will in just a bit," Sandy said. "I have to talk to Dusty."

"We didn't find anything or anybody at Tom's place," Dusty said. "Is that what you wanted to talk about, or are you planning again?"

"Come into the kitchen," she said, ignoring him for the moment. "But you know we have to do something before Sterling gets even more desperate." She heated more water in the microwave.

"You mean more than he is now?" Dusty asked as he sat at the table.

"Yes, more than he is now," she said. "Do you want a sandwich? Grandma always has something in the frig."

"Sure, and you can tell me your plan to entice them to Sapplehead."

Sandy found slices of a roast and made two sandwiches, sat at the table beside Dusty and told him what she'd been thinking. She feared Sterling already investigated the ranch and now it would be simple to terrorize her family. Her firsthand experience with the Englishman proved that he would go to any length to capture what he wanted and was certain that Sandy possessed his treasure.

"Sounds pretty weak, don't you think?" he said between bites of food.

"Do you have any ideas?" she asked. "Don't you think we have to do something?"

"Are you even certain this brooch is at your Sapplehead? Just because your grandfather left you that note doesn't mean you'll find it there."

"I know that's where it is. I'm just not sure where it is in the cabin, but I have an idea."

"Just like you're sure that car on the hill is Sterling," he said as he started eating the second sandwich.

"Oh, come on, Dusty. Of course, I'm not certain, but if it is, they'll surely follow us, won't they?"

"They usually do," Dusty said. "Do you have anything else to drink except tea?"

"Coffee?" she asked and when he nodded, she dropped instant coffee into the hot water. "Now what I was thinking," she said sitting beside him. "Tomorrow we can drive toward Sapplehead and see if they follow us. If they're anywhere around they'll probably come."

Dusty finished the second sandwich and sipped the coffee. "Shouldn't the police be in on this?"

"I'll call them before we leave and tell them the plan," Sandy said excitedly.

"It still sounds like a weak plan," Dusty said, shaking his head.

"Then do you have any suggestions?" she asked, studying his doubtful expression.

"I can't think of any," he said. "It may be all for nothing, you know, and the police will be pretty upset if they're called for something that doesn't even happen."

She banged her fist on the table. "But we have to do something. I don't want another night like this."

He rose, put his cup in the sink and turned to her. "Well, then, I guess it's a go."

"Yes," she said. "Tomorrow we go to Sapplehead."

Chapter 18

The next morning Sandy gazed at the eggs on her plate and smelled the odor of pancakes permeating the kitchen. Although today's plans didn't include a heavy breakfast, she knew the food on her plate should be eaten. She gazed across the table to Dusty and her father.

"I don't know if I can eat two eggs," she said.

Bradly nodded and forked more pancakes onto his plate. "Dusty tells me you're going to the cabin today."

"Yes," Sandy said as she poured syrup on her pancakes. "I think I know where grandfather would put that brooch."

"Well, if it's not under the floor, ask Danny. He's usually up there taking care of things." He took a bite of his pancake. "He may be a little slow, but he knows what goes on, alright."

"Does he still live in Centennial?" Sandy asked. "That's only a few miles from the cabin."

"Yes, he's still there. He works at a service station and doesn't miss a thing, so he'll know if those men have shown up there." Bradly pushed his plate away and pulled the cup of coffee closer. "You'll take the four wheel drive pickup up there. Remember how muddy it gets this time of year?"

Sandy recalled how spring was ushered in, cool and wet as the melting snow surged from the higher elevations. She ate one of the eggs as the yoke of the second one gazed at her. She pushed the plate aside and sipped the coffee. "What do I do with the brooch when I find it?" she asked her father.

"Whatever you want to do with it. Keep it, sell it, or give it back to the original British owners. They'll pay richly for it," Bradly said.

Sandy nodded but said nothing about her plan to lure Sterling to Sapplehead hoping he'd leave the family alone. She observed Dusty across the table eating one pancake after another. He winked at her and continued cleaning his plate. Her heart skipped a beat at his wink, and she couldn't help but smile. Why he didn't return to Colorado, she failed to ask. Actually, she wanted him here; for he understood the situation and she felt she could tell him anything. Right now, she'd rather not think about him leaving after this was over. How this would end, she dared not contemplate. If Sterling followed them to the cabin, she hoped the police would be close behind, but if things didn't go well, she and Dusty might find themselves in deep trouble. She sighed and rose from her chair.

"Are you about ready, Dusty?" she asked.

"All set to go," he said and finished the coffee in his cup.

"I'll get the pickup out of the garage," Bradly said. "Your grandmother fixed you a basket of sandwiches and drinks. It's there by the front door."

"Where is grandmother?" Sandy asked. "Doesn't she eat breakfast anymore?"

"She's already eaten and is probably out feeding her chickens. She's a ranch lady, you know."

Sandy nodded and followed him to the front door. Picking up the picnic basket, she stepped outside and surveyed the front yard, her gaze stopping on the rim of the hollow. Squinting, she checked the entire road east and west, but saw no car sitting anywhere along the way. She shook her head as Dusty stepped beside her.

"I don't see anyone up there," Sandy said. "Maybe the car I saw last night was someone else."

"Or maybe it's too early for them," Dusty said as he studied the rim. "It's only seven o'clock, you know."

"Do you suppose we should wait awhile?" she asked.

"Why wait?" he asked. "Let's get your brooch and leave the bad guys to the police. By the way did you call them?"

"Dad did. He was worried about us going up there alone," Sandy said as Bradly brought the pickup to the front yard.

"Then we're all set," Dusty said. "I guess you'd better drive, Sandy. I've no idea where we're going."

Sandy nodded and slipped behind the steering wheel when Bradly got out.

"You two be careful," Bradly said. "The law will be close behind and, really, I should go with you."

"No, Dad. Everything will be alright. Those guys probably aren't anywhere around here. They'd be lost out here in the wilds." She laughed nervously and shifted the four wheel drive into gear. "We'll be careful," she assured him. "We're just going to get the brooch and be right back. We'll probably be home in time for supper." She gazed at Dusty, who nodded in agreement, but his eyes disclosed anxiety.

Sandy let the clutch out and the pickup surged forward. She felt perspiration clinging to her hands and she wiped one then the other on her jeans. Nothing was said as Sandy urged the vehicle up the hill to the rim of the hollow. She gazed in both directions then pulled onto the two lane highway and turned west. Sighing at the emptiness of the road, she swallowed the lump that grew as they proceeded westward.

"Looks like nobody's here," she said. "Maybe Sterling wasn't watching after all."

"Could be," Dusty said. "We're probably a little paranoid."

"With good reason," Sandy said. "That experience would make anyone a little nuts."

He nodded in agreement and pointed to a small herd of deer watching them pass. "Looks like pretty good hunting," he said then turned to face her. "By the way, does your father have a gun in here?"

He checked for a rifle above the rear window. "Westerners usually have a gun for hunting hanging behind the seat."

"Dad usually doesn't carry a gun unless he's going hunting," she said as she slowed the pickup. "Check in the glove compartment just to make sure." She glanced at him as he slid wire cutters and a screw driver to one side of the enclosure then she drew her attention back to the road. "I never thought about a gun," she said.

"I should have," Dusty said as he slid his hand under the seat. "Nothing here except dust." He wiped his hand on his Levi's and looked out the window at the landscape changing from grassland to timbered hills. "This is really a long way from Chicago."

"It's just timber country. We're in the Snowy Range." She rolled down her window. "You can even smell the pine." Breathing deeply, she sighed at its sharpness. "It's so refreshing."

"Yes, it is, and chilly," he said. "Do you mind closing it?"

"Sure," she said, rolling up the glass. "Isn't it strange? It's like we're going on a pleasant trip to the woods."

"Maybe that's all it is," he said. "I wouldn't mind if that's all it was."

"Me too," she said. "But I can't wait to see the cabin again. I haven't been there since last summer and then I couldn't stay long because I had to get back for summer school to keep my teaching certificate current."

"That doesn't sound very exciting," he said.

"No, but it has to be done now and again." She glanced at him and smiled. "How about that book you're researching about ranching?"

He chuckled and crossed his arms. "It was going to be about cowboys. I thought some firsthand experience would make it more realistic. But now, I don't know. Maybe something else will come up."

"There's probably a lot to write about where you come from," she said. "I'll bet Chicago is exciting."

"Oh, yes." Dusty leaned back and gazed out the windshield. "But not as exciting as this. It might be a once in a lifetime experience."

"Hopefully the last time we experience it," she chuckled then pointed ahead. "There's what we're looking for. It's Centennial. I think I'll stop and see if Danny's working. He'll know if any strangers passed by."

"Not much of a town," Dusty said as they stopped at the service station. "Looks like you're out of it before you know it."

"It's pretty, though, don't you think?" She gestured at the pine clad hills surrounding the town.

"Oh, yeah, pretty," he said then pointed at the man approaching. "Is that Danny?"

"Oh, yes." Sandy smiled and rolled down the window. "Hi, Danny," she greeted the short, blond haired man dressed in bib overalls with a greasy red cloth hanging from his hip pocket.

"Sandy. I thought that was you. Are you heading for the cabin?" Danny asked.

"Yes," Sandy nodded. "Have you seen any strangers up here?"

"Just a couple guys." Danny pointed to the blue sedan sitting beside the gas pumps. "They're inside, just hanging around. They asked about you. Are they your friends?"

Sandy's gaze sped from the blue Buick to the large windows of the café and gift shop where she saw Sterling and Livingstone staring at them.

"Oh, boy," Sandy gasped. "They're here." She jammed the pickup into gear. "No, they're not friends, Danny. We're going to need the police. I hope they're behind us." She let the clutch out and as she turned the pickup onto the highway, she saw Sterling and Livingstone rush from the building.

Chapter 19

Bradly Templeton cleared the breakfast plates from the table and stacked them beside the sink that Lily filled with warm sudsy water.

"I still think we should have a dish washer," he told Lily.

"We have one. No, we have two," Lily said. "You and me." She lowered the plates into the water. "Now grab the dish towel and do your part."

Bradly did so, drying and stacking the dishes in the cupboard and waiting for Lily to wash the large frying pan she used for baking pancakes. "I should have gone with them," he said as he grabbed the frying pan. "Sandy seemed to want to go alone with her young fellow."

"Well, of course she did. Don't you remember being young?" She snatched the dish towel from him. "Don't dry the frying pan with that."

He released the towel and pan. "I wasn't thinking about romance. I have a feeling they're going to the cabin for another reason entirely."

"Oh, you mean to keep those men away from us," Lily said nonchalantly. "That's what she's doing, you know."

"Yeah, Mom, I know," Bradly said as he wrung the dish cloth and wiped the table. "I just hope the police have caught them or they've given up and gone back to England."

"Now you're wishing on a star," Lily said. "What they've planned is too much to give up." She chuckled. "They just didn't realize what a complicated mess they were getting into when they began their treasure hunt."

"They'll have a little trouble trying to follow Sandy to the cabin with a car." He carefully folded the dish cloth and hung it on the three pronged hanger above the sink. "It's pretty muddy around the creek."

"I hope Sandy can make it. She hasn't driven that road for a while, and she usually rides along with your dad." Lily folded the dish towel, gave it a pat and hung it beside the dish cloth.

"She'll do alright and Dusty's with her."

"He's a nice guy, but they don't seem to be serious about each other, as yet, anyway." She untied her apron and hung it in its place beside the sink.

"She could do worse. She could bring home an educator," he laughed. "He wouldn't be much help around here."

"That's really what I expected, her being a school teacher," Lily said, then stopped as she heard the phone ringing.

"I'll get that," Bradly said. "I wish Sandy could have taken a cell phone with her, but nothing works up there." He picked up the phone. "Hello, Bradly Templeton here. What? Oh, hello, Danny. What's going on?" He gazed at Lily as he listened. "Okay, Danny, calm down. I'll take care of it." He returned the receiver to its cradle. "Sandy and Dusty stopped at Centennial and those guys were there. She'll probably make a mad dash for Sapplehead. She can lose them up there in the mud."

'What are you going to do? You'd better call the police." Lily wrung her hands as she gazed at him.

"Yes, I'll do that," he said reaching for the phone. "But they'll have to take the long way around or they'll get mired down in the mud, too." He dialed the number and explained the situation. "If you come to the ranch, I'll lead the way up there." He waited for their decision then nodded. "Okay, come quickly. They shouldn't be hard to catch up there in that soft mud." Pushing the button, to get a dial tone, he said to Lily. "A couple more calls and I'll be on my way." He dialed again and waited. "Oh, Tom. We have a situation at the cabin. Bring your four wheel drive and come over here." He took a deep breath. "And bring a couple guns."

"Oh, Bradly, will it come to that?" Lily asked.

"I hope not," Bradly said. "One more call." He dialed once more and stood on one foot then the other. "Yes, Bradly Templeton here. I'd like to speak with Sergeant Cooper." Waiting again, he felt Lily tug on his shirt sleeve.

"Are you calling in the army?" she asked.

"Air force," he said. "Cooper owes me one."

"They can't do anything." Lily's eyes brightened. "Can they?"

"We'll see," Bradly said. "The only thing that can get up there fast would be a helicopter. It can land on the meadow right there outside the cabin." He waited nervously moving from one foot to the other. "Hello, Coop. I have an assignment for you." As he explained, Bradly's eyebrows narrowed then raised. "Okay. You know where the cabin is. Yes, I know you'll do what you can. Yes, Tom and I are leaving right now. We'll have to take the long way so the police car can get through. Muddy up there this time of year, you know." He stopped a moment as Tom entered. "Okay, do what you can," he said into the receiver then returned it to its cradle.

"You ready?" Tom asked. "The police car's waiting outside."

"Let's do it," Bradly said.

"Are you sure Lance Cooper can help?" Lily asked.

"He's been hunting up here every year. Yes, if he can get through the red tape, he'll be there," Bradly said. "I just hope he can get hold of a helicopter."

"That's asking a lot," Tom said. "It's not a military situation."

"We have to take the police the long way in. They'll never make it through the mud in that cruiser. A helicopter is all I could think of."

Tom shrugged. "There's only one policeman in that cruiser. He can ride with us, and we can carry the bad guys in the back of the pickup."

"Look again," Bradly said pointing out the kitchen window. "There's three cruisers out there."

"Oh, boy." Tom shook his head "They must want those fellows pretty bad."

"Or they know something we don't," Bradly said.

"Looks like we go the long way around to the cabin," Tom said.

"Yeah." Bradly nodded and moved to the door. "Let's get those guys once and for all."

Chapter 20

The morning sun sent long spears of light through the timber on both sides of the road. Sandy studied the dirt trails leading off the highway and into the shaded stands of Lodge pole and Ponderosa pine.

"I know it's one of these roads right along here," Sandy said, puzzled that all the exists looked the same. It had been some time since she looked for the turn off. She was fifteen or sixteen the last time she went with Grandpa. After that her interests turned away from fishing and hiking the mountain paths. Now all she could see were mosquitoes, ticks and carrying water from the spring. The magic of childhood disappeared into adolescence.

"You're certain the road is right along here?" Dusty asked as he gazed through the rear window. "They're catching up."

"There it is," she said as she recognized a jeep trail partially grown over with grass sneaking between the trees and out of sight as it turned and twisted through the forest.

"It's right there. That jeep trail is the road to Sapplehead," she said as she turned the pickup down the bumpy road. An old comfortable feeling combined with her anticipation as she remembered riding with her grandfather over the invisible trail. She felt the tracks were leading her home. It was a place where she could forget the death of her grandfather and her mother. Sapplehead remained a place where she could leave the world behind and be a child again.

They bumped over the rocks in the trail and splashed through the muddy places, the truck's tires singing a slippery song as they grabbed for traction in the low meadows flooded by snow melting on the slopes above them.

She eased across the wet meadow and sighed with relief as the pickup's tires gripped the dry, rocky road leading upward through the pines and gritted her teeth as the rocks scraped the underside of the four wheel drive. She didn't remember the road being so rocky, but then, Grandpa's Jeep had bounded over the road with ease. She watched the trail carefully, remembering a turn off they must take and scooted forward in the seat.

"We have to turn up here. See? Lightning struck that tree, and we turn just on the other side. Are Sterling and Livingstone still behind us?"

"Yes, but I don't know how they made it this far. Sterling must be a good driver. I thought we lost them when we crossed that wet little park, but he barreled right through it." Dusty shook his head. "I can't even drive that good."

"That's what he does for a living," Sandy said as she neared the broken tree. "He's a chauffeur."

"I'll bet he never drove on a road like this," Dusty chuckled. "That car's going to be a wreck." He brought his attention forward. "Is this the tree you were taking about?" He pointed out the window.

"Yes," Sandy said. "Now we go down a long rocky hill, round the bend and you'll be able to see the cabin."

"Sapplehead," Dusty chuckled.

"Yes, Sapplehead." Sandy sighed as the image sent a warm feeling through her.

"And this must be the long rocky hill." Dusty grabbed the side of the seat as the pickup's hood pointed down the steep slope. "I wonder what Sterling is thinking right now." He chuckled at the thought.

"This hill won't be his only concern." Sandy nodded ahead. "That will probably stop him."

Dusty gasped at the swollen stream ahead of them. "I'm a little concerned, myself."

"Hang on tight," Sandy said. "We have to ram right through."

The four wheel drive fish tailed as Sandy hit the soft mud on the stream's bank, but caught traction on its rocky bottom. She gritted her teeth and tightened her hold on the steering wheel as the pickup's tires spun and she swallowed a lump in her throat as the four wheel drive attacked the opposite shore which was muddier and slipperier than the decent into the stream. She held her breath as the pickup ate away at the slimy dirt and noticed Dusty pushing on the dashboard, helping all he could. As they reached solid ground, Sandy stopped the pickup to catch her breath.

"Are they still coming?" she asked.

"They're on the other side of the water," Dusty said. "This should be a sight to see. Sterling's getting out of the car to take a look." He opened the window. "Listen. You can hear them talking."

"I'm sure we can make it if it isn't too deep," Sterling said as he walked to the stream.

Sandy watched him sink into the mud that extended outward from the stream's bank. She smiled remembering Grandpa telling her the cabin was almost inaccessible in the spring because of the swollen stream. She sat back in the seat wondering if the police could make it even this far.

Sterling returned to his car and slammed the door. A determined look covered his face as he studied the road block before him. Carefully he backed up then jammed the car into gear.

Sandy watched intently as the car hit the mud, its motor roaring and wheels spinning. The tires finally caught on the stream's rocky bottom and Sandy giggled as the car surged through the water up to the doors. She noticed Livingstone push on the dashboard as the heavy car reached the far bank and began to spin in the mud. Its front tires reached for the dry dirt beyond, squealing as if in pain. Then the car stopped as the tires spun in the soft earth.

Sterling rocked the car back and forth, but it refused to fight the mud and sat spinning its tires. The man banged on the steering wheel then shut off the motor.

Sandy watched them climb from the car stepping in the oozing mud as they rushed toward dry land. She giggled softly when Sterling's shoe stayed in the mud as he leaped toward the solid surface and laughed out loud when he reached for the shoe, lost his footing, and fell into the soft soggy earth. Even if he killed her, this one event would make the going easier. As she watched Livingstone pull Sterling from the mud, she realized her greatest desire would be to see Livingstone fall in after him.

But Livingstone didn't. His short, stocky arm pulled the muddy, cursing Sterling to safety, and as they started up the hill, Sterling brushed at his suit with his handkerchief.

"Bloody land," he shouted. "Let's get that brooch and get out of this country."

"I think it's time we got out of here, too," Dusty said. "They're on the move."

Sandy shoved the pickup into gear and increased her speed as they rounded the bend then she slowed down at the sight of the cabin tucked among the pines. It stood in a wide shaft of sunlight squeezing among the trees and spreading out as the land opened onto a large grassy meadow. A deer, drinking from the stream, lifted its antlered head and bounded into the forest as they approached.

Sandy gazed in the rear view mirror as she urged the pickup across the meadow. "Do you see them coming?" she asked Dusty.

"No, not yet. They probably drive better than they walk," he laughed. "Maybe they'll get lost between there and here."

"Not if they follow the road. Sterling's a pretty good tracker. Remember?" she reminded him.

As she stopped in front of the cabin, her thoughts flooded with memories of the familiar surroundings. She smiled as she recollected catching her first fish and how the cabin became known as Sapplehead. She blinked back the sweet tears of the memory as Dusty tugged on her arm.

"Come on now. No time for that. Let's get your brooch and get out before they get here," Dusty said. "Come on."

Chapter 21

Sandy slowly opened the door of the cabin and stepped inside. Its familiar wood smoke odor overwhelmed her, and she surveyed her childhood playground. She remembered it being roomy, but now it appeared small and cramped. Two curtainless windows above the worn couch allowed the sun's rays to splash onto the wooden floor and stream to the wood burning stove, its dusty, rusted pipe extending through the roof.

"Looks like someone's been here," Dusty said as he picked up an empty vegetable can.

"Hunters use it," Sandy said. "They don't clean up after themselves very well."

"Okay now, your father said something about the brooch being under the floor." Dusty pulled back an old braided rug. "Is this it?" He nodded at the piece of flooring that didn't match the rest of the pine strips.

"Yes," Sandy said. She dropped to her knees and pulled at the board. "It doesn't seem to want to move." As she gritted her teeth and yanked again, the wood came away in her hand and as she carefully reached for the tin box hidden beneath, she heard footsteps at the open doorway.

Sterling filled the opening and Livingstone pushed his way inside. "So, this is where you've hidden it," Sterling said rushing to her and grabbing the box. "Finally, I'll have it."

Sandy watched him yank the tin box open and held her hand over her mouth to keep from yelling as he dumped the contents onto the worn wooden table. She gasped as all that fell out were three fishing lures and fishing weights. She heard Sterling sigh then turn to her.

"There's nothing here but fishing stuff," he growled. "Where's the brooch?"

"I don't know." She pointed to the tin box. "That's where it's supposed to be." She cringed when he drew a gun from his pocket. "Grandpa left a note saying it would be here."

"Let's see the note," Sterling ordered.

Sandy felt in her jacket pocket and handed him the brooch with the blue stone.

"That's it," Livingstone said. "Let me see it." He grabbed the brooch and studied it. "It's lovely. See Sterling? I believe this is it."

Sandy watched his eyes brighten then turn dim as his eyebrows lowered.

"No," He shook his head. "The brooch had a ruby. This isn't a ruby."

"Where's the note?" Sterling asked grabbing the brooch from Livingstone.

"It's inside. Pull the little latch and you'll see it," Sandy said.

Sterling did so and the piece of paper fell out. Retrieving it from the floor, he opened it and stared at Sandy. "What does this mean? Sapplehead?"

Sandy felt her palms sweating and waved her arm around the room. "This is Sapplehead. This cabin is called Sapplehead."

"Then the brooch is here somewhere," Livingstone concluded as he gazed around the room. "It's in this cabin somewhere."

"That's what the note says." Sandy sighed and wiped her hands on her jeans. "But I don't know where."

"Then we'll just have to find it," Sterling said.

Sandy growled at the men going through the roughhewn cupboards and gasped as the chipped porcelain plates fell to the wooden floor. The cushions of the old, tattered easy chair seemed to groan beneath the knife in Livingstone's hand. He dumped the knives, forks, and spoons from the drawer onto the table and carefully searched the container for a secret compartment.

Sandy gazed wide eyed at the combined kitchen, living room and shook her head angrily. "Look at what you're doing to this place." She rushed at Livingstone and grabbed his arm. "Stop. You're destroying everything."

Livingstone pushed her aside and continued his work. "All you have to do is tell us where the brooch is. We'd gladly stop."

Where would Grandpa hide the brooch? Her gazed followed the path of the sun's ray's to the heavy table, the worn braided brown rug beneath it to the closet with no door where Grandpa kept his fishing equipment.

"I don't know where it is," she finally said. "Grandpa could have hidden it anywhere."

Her gaze settled on the closed door to the bedroom. "Maybe in the bedroom," she suggested. "Or between the logs." She pointed to the rough logs cemented tightly together. "I really don't know."

Sterling took Sandy by the arm. "You and the cowboy search the bedroom. The brooch must be somewhere in this cabin."

Sandy watched Sterling pull the stove pipe from the back of the stove and carefully take it outside. She smiled and stepped into the bedroom behind Dusty. "The only thing he'll find in the stovepipe is soot."

Dusty nodded and gazed around the bedroom. Its double bed had been neatly straightened by its last occupants and a half melted candle leaned sideward from a tuna fish can. Dusty sat on the dark green woolen blanket that stretched across the sagging mattress. "A cozy little place," he said. "Did you come here often?"

"When I was a kid, I did," Sandy said pulling a drawer from the chest. "I used to love it up here."

"I can see why." Dusty bounced on the dilapidated mattress. "It could be a nice summer place."

"Better get busy," Sandy ordered. "We're not here on a pleasure outing, you know."

Dusty surveyed the room. "Got any ideas where I should busy myself?"

"Just look anywhere," Sandy said as she slid the drawer back into the chest and pulled out the next one. She squealed at the mouse that jumped from the drawer of shredded cloth, raced across the floor and under the bed.

"That's one reason it stopped being fun up here," she said and gingerly pulled the shredded cloth from the drawer. She looked around the room and stepped to the clothes closet, its door a tattered blanket hanging in the opening. She jerked the curtain aside, stepped inside and stood on tiptoe to gaze on the shelf above the broom handle hanger rod. Running her hand along the dusty shelf, she grunted at the mouse droppings.

"Nothing here," she said. "I don't understand. Grandpa wouldn't put it in a place so hard to find." She stepped back into the bedroom and tried to stop tears pushing from her eyes. "What do we do, Dusty? It isn't here. It just isn't here. And those guys are getting more anxious. They think I know where the brooch is and I'm not telling them." She wiped her face with her hand. "How are we going to get out of this?"

"We'll get through this." He held her and rocked to and fro. "How about another plan?" His gaze stopped on the two windows above the bed. "Hey, now wait. How about crawling out the window and making a break for the pickup?"

Sandy drew herself from the comfort of his arms and looked at the windows. Stepping onto the bed, she unlocked the clasp holding the two small windows together and pulled them open.

The warm piney air rushed in carrying the songs of the bluebird and high country jays. Sandy's gaze roamed the familiar sight of the outhouse and tool shed Grandpa had attached to it. Closing the windows, she turned back to Dusty, her eyes full of hope.

"We can run to the tool shed," she said jumping from the bed. "There may be a shovel or something to use against them."

"Now it's farm implements against guns?" he asked.

"What else can we do?"

"I think we should make a dash for the pickup and get out of here," Dusty said. "Do you have the keys?"

"They're in the ignition," she said starting toward the window.

Sterling's voice stopped her. "Have you found anything?" he asked.

Sandy emphatically shook her head. "We were just starting on the bed," she said grabbing the saggy mattress.

Sterling stepped forward and helped her shove it from the broken springs. He felt the lumps then split them with a knife. Carefully he cut and searched each bulge then threw the knife disgustedly. "Where is the brooch?" he shouted.

"I don't know," Sandy said, her voice shaking. "I really don't know."

Sterling angrily pulled the drawers from the chest and reexamined where Sandy already searched.

Sandy felt tenseness throughout the cabin. Not a sound came from the kitchen. She watched Sterling tear the chest of drawers apart and kick the splintered boards then he stopped and listened to the silence coming from the other room. He pushed Sandy and Dusty ahead of him from the bedroom.

"He's found it," Sterling said shoving them aside. "Livingstone's found it."

Livingstone sat at the table, breathing deeply.

"What is it?" Sterling asked. "What's going on?"

"Just taking a sit down," Livingstone said. "Did you find it? You look like you've found it."

"You stopped looking," Sterling said. "You're just sitting there in that chair. Have you found it and hidden it away?"

"You're the one who looks guilty." Livingstone glared at his partner. "How do I know you didn't find it?"

"If I had, I'd be gone and you'd be dead," Sterling said coldly.

"And if I had it, I'd just be gone," Livingstone yelled.

Sandy gently pulled on the sleeve of Dusty's Levi jacket. Slowly they stepped toward the bedroom.

"And them." Livingstone brought his attention to Sandy and Dusty. "They were alone in there. They could have found it."

Sandy stopped her movement, and they shook their heads to answer Livingstone.

"There's nothing in there," Sterling confirmed. He gazed at Livingstone's angry face. "You *did* find it."

"No," Livingstone screamed. He shook his finger at Sterling. "I believe you have it."

"You're a liar." Sterling moved his hand to the gun inside his jacket, but Livingstone jumped onto him before he could draw the weapon.

With all the men's attention drawn to each other, Sandy pulled Dusty toward the bedroom.

"Stop," Livingstone shouted and jerked at Sterling's collar. "No one has the brooch, and we can't find it by fighting each other."

Sandy stopped beside the bedroom door when Livingstone turned to face her.

"Where else could it be?" he asked her calmly.

Sandy noticed the distrust lingering on Sterling's face and Livingstone trying to assume an air of innocence. Could Livingstone have found it? Yes, Livingstone looked like the cat that caught the goldfish. She shook her head at him.

"I just don't know," she finally told him.

Sterling sighed and glanced around the room, surveying the room's overturned chairs, the stovepipe torn from the stove and the cupboards filled with broken dishes.

"It has to be here," he said. "If this is Sapplehead, it has to be here." He stared at Sandy. "You wouldn't lead us astray, would you?"

"No." Sandy wiped her moist palms on her jeans. "This is Sapplehead."

"Then we just have to search more carefully." Sterling strode back to the cupboard and flung the shattered dishes to the floor.

Livingstone glared at him then resumed poking his knife between the log walls then Sandy watched him force the sturdy legs from the table and chairs hoping each one might be hollow and contain the valued gem. She felt a sharp pain flash through her chest. It could not hurt much more if it had been her legs. Gazing at the cabin that once held only joy and comfort, she felt the hair on the back of her neck raise in anger.

Everything he held dear had been smashed and ruined. If only she could use those table legs on them. Her eyes widened as she gazed at the men checking each leg carefully.

"It isn't here," Sterling said and disgustedly flung the chair leg across the room then spun to face Livingstone. "Of course not, because you have it. There's no sense looking further." He pulled the gun from his coat. "I'll have it now."

Sandy felt the hushed terror filling the room. All attention turned toward Sterling's gun as she took a step backward toward the bedroom.

Sterling saw the movement and moved the gun from Livingstone to Sandy. That instant Livingstone rushed forward and knocked the weapon from his hand. As the gun slid across the floor, both men scrambled for it and Livingstone retrieved it.

"Hold it right there, Sterling. There'll be no more of this. We're here to find the brooch not to kill each other."

Sandy stepped into the bedroom, Dusty quickly following. She gasped when Sterling grabbed Livingstone pinning his arms to his sides and twisted his arms until the gun fell to the floor. Livingstone stomped on Sterling's foot and jabbed him with his elbow forcing

Sterling to release him then pounded the man with his fists, but Sterling twisted and turned rendering the blows powerless.

Sandy held her hand over her open mouth. Her heart pounded and she stood frozen watching Sterling hit Livingstone relentlessly. She gasped behind her hand and watched Livingstone fall and lay silent on the rough wooden floor. Her gaze met Sterling's as he searched his partner's pockets then picked up the gun lying beside Livingstone's still form.

She felt Dusty pull her into the bedroom, shut the door and shove her toward the window. He turned the latch and flung the panes open.

"Hurry," he said. "There's no time left. Sterling will kill us all." He heaved her toward the opening.

Sandy couldn't stop the tears of fear and anger rushing to her eyes. She blinked them away and flashed a look toward the closed door. She scrambled through the opening and stood shaking while Dusty jumped head first through the window landing beside her.

They ran toward the shed as two shots zinged past them. Darting behind the shed, they stood panting and holding each other tightly waiting for eternity.

"I think he killed Livingstone," Sandy said, hiding her face in Dusty's chest. "Now he's coming after us."

The late morning sun streamed through the trees across the meadow as Sandy studied the distance to the safety of the timber.

"We have to get to the woods," she said. "Maybe we can lose him there."

Dusty nodded and chanced a peek around the corner of the shed. He pulled his head back like a turtle's disappearing into its shell.

"He's coming around the backside of the cabin. We can't even get into the shed to get the farm implements," he said.

Sandy surveyed the land beyond the outhouse. The stream babbled over the rocks and across the water, the timber stood dense and shadowy.

"Let's try for the stream," she said. "We can hide in the woods on the other side." She stepped carefully along the wall of the outhouse. "It's not far. Come on."

Dusty gazed at her then nodded. "Let's do it," he whispered.

They dashed from the protection of the outhouse and raced toward the stream. Splashing into its swift coldness, they pulled each other against the current.

Sandy turned and saw Sterling step from behind the outhouse. "Hurry," she screamed. "He sees us."

She gasped as Sterling aimed the deadly weapon.

Chapter 22

Sandy felt the icy chill of the swollen mountain stream seep into her western boots and the warm rays of the June sun on her back. The clean piney air filed her lungs as she gasped at Sterling carefully aiming his gun. Her gaze flashed from Sterling to the woods beyond that seemed the only refuge. She started to race for her life, but Dusty grabbed her arm and jerked her toward boulders jutting from the middle of the stream.

"Come on," he yelled over the angry water. "We're sitting ducks here."

Sandy felt the buzz of the bullets zipping by her head then the cold water come up to meet her as she fell behind the large stone. She pulled herself to her knees as water rushed around her and hung onto Dusty as he peered above the rock.

"He's walking down the bank. I believe he thinks he's killed us," Dusty said as he ducked his head behind the rock. "Let's run for the woods." He motioned toward the stand of timber on the far bank and slowly moved from the boulder's protection, his gaze remaining on Sterling as he helped Sandy to her feet in the water's current.

They splashed toward the river's bank, fighting the current's desire to pull them off their feet. Step after agonizing step they clung to each other, their boots sliding on the slippery rocks on the stream's bed.

On the bank, Sandy stopped to rub the feeling into her legs that the icy water left numb and wanted to linger in the sunlight that bathed the shore, but Dusty jerked her toward the trees.

"Sterling's spotted us," he said. "He's crossing the creek."

Sandy glanced at the opposite bank and saw Sterling gingerly stepping into the icy water. She stumbled toward the protection of the trees as her numbed feet and legs began to tingle and she stopped behind a tree to rub them.

Dusty peered toward the stream then looked anxiously at Sandy. "Come on. You know how good he is at tracking."

Sandy gave her soggy feet a shake and gazed through the forest before her. "There's a cave up here. Jackie and I used to play there. It didn't seem far from the cabin."

She took the lead, pushing branches aside and rushing through the wild shooting star flowers and buttercups. Her gaze searched the timbered hill for the cave in the rocky upheavals.

Shots rang out as they slipped among the sunshine and shadows. Sandy flinched at the bullet hitting the tree beside her and slipped behind the rocks protruding from the forest carpet.

"The cave's at the top of this hill," Sandy said as she gasped for breath. "If Sterling sees us enter, it won't do any good to go up there. He'll have us penned in."

"You want to wait for him? Plenty of sticks and stones here," he said.

Sandy had to grin at the twinkle in his eyes. "How about the cornered cat plan?" she asked.

"Well, we can't run forever," Dusty reminded her. "He's too good at tracking." He picked up a branch. "I think it's time for the cat plan."

"Against the bullets?" she asked. "We can't." She stopped, realizing she sounded like him at the river on the outskirts of Laramie. She finally sighed and nodded. "Okay, I guess we did it before. Sort of."

Dusty chuckled. "Sort of? Why, we had him on the run." He peeked around the rock. "I don't see him. You don't suppose he's lost?"

Sandy's expression confirmed his thoughts. "Of course not," he concluded.

Sandy picked up a club and leaned against the rock. "You guard your side of the rock and "I'll watch this one."

They turned from each other, clubs raised, waiting for Sterling to step around the stone.

Sandy felt a cramp twisting the muscles in her arms but dared not lower her weapon. She gritted her teeth when a movement beyond the hiding place attracted her attention. Silently she lowered the club and pulled on Dusty's jacket as she pointed above them at Sterling approaching the cave.

A smile pushed the seriousness from Dusty's face when Sterling entered the cave. "We can get him when he comes out," he whispered.

Sandy followed him, sneaking from stone to stone, until they stood beside the cave's entrance. Dusty lifted his club waiting for the gunman to exit and Sandy stood beside him, ready to execute a second blow if necessary.

They waited. Dusty finally lowered the club. "Is there another exit?" he asked.

Sandy shook her head then stood stone still. Sterling stood above the cave, his evil smile sending a cold chill through her.

"He must have come out while we were sneaking up," she said poking Dusty to look above them.

"The cave will be a dandy grave," Sterling said, climbing from his perch.

Sandy watched his gun waver when he hopped from the rocks toward them. *It's now or never,* she thought as she rushed toward Sterling, swinging the club at him.

The blow hit Sterling in the stomach and he folded. Dusty finished him by swinging his branch at the lowered head. Sterling crumbled and lay silent in the soft carpet of the forest.

Dusty dropped the club and dusted his hands together. "Looks like that'll finish him. Now what? We can get to the pickup and get out of here."

Sandy dropped her branch beside Sterling. "Maybe the police are there. Oh, I hope so," she said as she started down the incline.

"I don't see how they could be. Sterling's car is blocking the road," Dusty said as he stepped behind her. "And we have to be careful because Livingstone's still in the cabin."

She stopped short. "Oh, yes. I forgot about him. I wonder if he's alive."

"We can't be sure," Dusty said. "It seemed that Sterling had the only gun, but we can't be sure of that either."

As they descended through the timber without a backward glance, Sandy didn't notice Sterling rub his head, pull himself to his feet and pick up his gun before he wilted back into the needled carpet.

"We should have taken Sterling's gun," Dusty said as they neared the stream.

"I don't think he'll be able to use it," Sandy said. "He should be resting for quite a while. We'll be gone by the time he wakes up."

"I hope so." Dusty shook his head. "I don't like him behind us awake or asleep."

Sandy nodded and continued down the steep slope then stopped, leaned against a boulder, and gazed up the hill. "He's not coming is he?"

Dusty surveyed the path they had taken. "I don't see anyone, but you don't see him until he's here." He stepped onto the invisible path leading to the cabin. "I sure wish we'd taken his gun."

Sandy studied the woods and nodded. "I guess I wish that, too," she said as she moved behind him. "He looked pretty disabled when we left him." She glanced over her shoulder. "You don't suppose we should go back and get it."

She heard him chuckle and wished she'd said nothing about the weapon.

"I think the saying is something about letting sleeping dogs lie," he said. "I'm sure that dog would reach up and bite you."

"Yes," she agreed. "Yes, I'm sure you're right." She looked backward again. "Let's just get as far away from Sterling as we can."

"Fine by me," Dusty said. "There's the stream. Are you ready for another cold dunking?"

"Ready as I'll ever be," she said as she stopped at the water and looked toward the cabin. "It looks quiet enough. I wonder if Livingstone is waiting in there."

"Only one way to find out," Dusty said as he took her by the hand. "Come on. Let's get to that pickup."

Chapter 23

Sandy plunged into the frigid water holding tightly to Dusty's hand and gritted her teeth as the water surged above her knees leaving her skin painful and numb. She wanted to stop and rub life into her limbs, but Dusty pulled her relentlessly against the powerful current.

"Come on," he urged. "Don't stop now. We're almost there."

Forcing one foot in front of the other, Sandy let herself be yanked and toed through the knee high rapids. She could see the bank of the river and surged forward, forcing her numb limbs to obey. The meadow and cabin were within sight when Sandy slipped on a stone landing full length in the water. She would certainly have been carried downstream if Dusty hadn't pulled her to her feet.

"Come on," he said. "No time for swimming."

Sandy felt hot anger at his insensitiveness, but her outrage warmed her, and she stepped forward much easier. He did that on purpose, she knew. Just to keep her going.

The river bank was so welcome that Sandy would willingly have kissed the ground, but Dusty urged her to the edge of the meadow.

"There's the pickup," he said, panting and rubbing his legs. "I don't see anyone around the cabin."

"What do we do, just make a dash for the truck?" she asked, gazing across the wide grassy park.

"Let's make a run for the tool shed. That's about half way to the cabin," Dusty suggested as he grabbed her hand. "Come on. Let's do it."

She felt herself traveling faster than her legs actually wanted to move but held tightly to Dusty's hand as he sped across the meadow to the shed and outhouse.

Panting, she stopped behind the wooden wall of the outhouse. "Shell we get farm implements from the shed while we're here?"

"It wouldn't hurt," Dusty answered. "As far as I know, Livingstone doesn't have a gun."

Inside the tool shed, Sandy heaved a sigh of relief. Somehow she felt safe away from the open meadow. She shivered in her wet clothes as she observed the familiar shed. Sunbeams speared through the boards that made up the walls and a fly buzzed in the shaft of light. The building smelled of wood and clean dirt and Sandy welcomed the homey warmth seeping through her.

"Why'd your grandfather attach this to the outhouse?" Dusty asked. "It seems silly to me."

"I guess it worked for Grandpa," Sandy said. "Anyway, it gives us more walls to hide behind."

He nodded in agreement. "Okay," he said, pointing at the wall. "Do you want the shovel or a hammer?"

Sandy stared at the wall. Most of her grandfather's tools were missing from the nails he'd hammered to hold the implements. "Dad must have taken them to the ranch," she finally said. "I'll take the hammer."

Dusty grabbed the shovel and Sandy followed him outside around the corner of the shed.

"I don't see anything moving at the cabin," she said as she held the hammer, ready to pound anything that came close.

"Okay." Dusty securely held the shovel and stepped from the shed's protective walls. "Let's go."

She raced after him, her gaze shifting from the cabin to the safety of the pickup. Still nothing moved from the building as she jumped into the truck, her gaze on the cabin's doorway. As Dusty slid into the passenger seat, she reached for the keys she'd left in the ignition.

"What are you waiting for?" Dusty asked. "Let's go."

Sandy gazed out the windshield and surveyed the meadow. "They're gone," she said slowly. "Somebody took the keys."

"Maybe they fell out." Dusty groped on the floor of the pickup, feeling for what he hoped would be there.

Sandy frantically checked her pockets then gazed at Dusty. "He took them. Sterling took the keys." She banged the steering wheel and fought tears forming in her eyes.

"Well," Dusty said as he took a deep breath. "He doesn't want us driving out."

Sandy gazed at him and tried to smile. "Apparently not. I guess we're in for some more walking unless you learned how to hot wire like they do in the movies."

He shook his head and smiled. "My gang didn't go in for that type of education." He studied the cabin door and motioned to it. "Do you suppose we should check on Livingstone? I'm a bit curious."

"I'm right behind you," Sandy said as she opened the pickup door. "I'm sure we'd all like to know."

Dusty stopped when he reached the cabin door. "Okay. You got the hammer?"

She held up the tool and nodded then felt her heart jump to her throat as Dusty slowly and carefully opened the door.

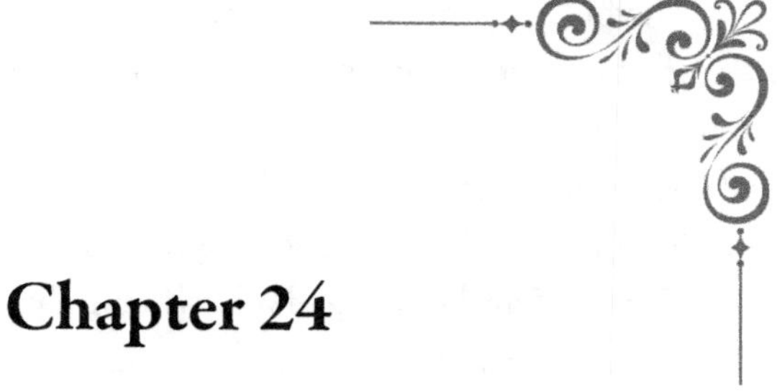

Chapter 24

Sandy followed Dusty into the cabin and held the hammer above her head expecting Livingstone to attack if he were still alive. Only an eerie silence greeted her.

"You stay here," Dusty said. "I'll check the bedroom."

Sandy nodded and rubbed the goose bumps forming on her arms as she surveyed the destruction the brooch caused. She wished she'd not led Sterling to Sapplehead, but if she hadn't the men might have done something more drastic. She shivered at the thought and at the coolness of the cabin that made her damp clothes cling to her body. Her stomach growled and she remembered the second egg she didn't eat. Was breakfast so long ago? She checked her watch. Only ten thirty. She felt certain days instead of hours had passed. No police came. Were they stuck behind Sterling's car and were walking to the cabin? They should be here by now. She gazed out the open door to the wide meadow, but nothing moved across the dark green park. As she laid the hammer on the table, she saw the brooch with the blue stone winking at her as the shaft of sunlight caught its sheen. She picked it up and opened it, searching for more information that it might contain. Only the photographs of her grandma and grandpa peered at her. The only clue was Sapplehead and that lead them nowhere. She sighed and slipped the brooch into her jacket pocket as Dusty returned from the bedroom.

"There's no one here," he said shrugging his shoulders. "He must have taken off walking."

"Maybe he went back to Sterling's car thinking he could get it out of the mud," Sandy said. "Or perhaps he's lost in the woods somewhere."

"That car might be a good idea," Dusty said snapping his fingers. "I wonder if he left the keys in the ignition."

"What?" Sandy asked. "Now what are you planning?"

"If we can get that car out of the mud, we can drive it out of here." Dusty rushed to the open door. "Come on," he urged.

"But if they couldn't, how can we get it out?" she asked as she hurried to keep up with him.

"We're more determined," he said, taking her by the hand and rushing across the meadow.

"Why are we in such a hurry?" she asked, stumbling after him.

"I don't know," he said, slowing his pace. "I'm just ready to get out of here."

Sandy nodded. "Me, too."

"Then let's do it." Dusty lengthened his stride and Sandy trotted to keep up.

"Maybe the police are there." Sandy hoped more than actually expected that event to occur.

"That would make my day," he said.

As Sandy followed across the meadow and onto the road through the timber, she stopped and gazed back toward the meadow. All appeared so calm, so pleasant and pleasing, as if nothing dramatic happened there at all. Sighing, she turned from the scene and hustled to catch Dusty striding ahead of her.

The warmth of the morning intensified, and Sandy rubbed her wet clothes as they dried in the early summer breeze. As she patted her jacket she felt the blue stoned brooch. She drew it from her pocket and studied it again. Although she turned it over, opened it and gazed at the photos, nothing new appeared. The ruby brooch simply wasn't at Sapplehead. Grandfather must have moved it after he put the note inside the fake brooch was all she could conclude. This whole episode was a waste of time. Perhaps someone using the cabin took it. She sighed and increased her speed to catch Dusty whose attention was concentrated on the blue car ahead of him, stuck in the mud.

"There it is," he yelled back to her. "Come on. Hurry it up."

Running at his command, Sandy felt her heart beating wildly at the chance of escape. Then she stopped short and gazed first at Sterling's car then studied the empty road behind it where she hoped a police car might be parked. Discouragement replaced the elation and she sighed, forcing back tears swelling up and spilling down her checks. Shaking her head, she wiped her face and stepped beside Dusty.

"Is anyone in it?" she asked.

"It all looks pretty quiet," he said as he cautiously approached the car and stepped into the mud surrounding the tires.

"Are the keys there?" she asked.

"Well, what do you know? They are." Dusty opened the door and slipped behind the steering wheel. "I wonder if it will start." Turning the key, he chuckled as the motor purred like an oversized cat.

Sandy stepped back as Dusty put it into gear and began rocking it back and forth. She folded her arms and shook her head at the impossible task he asked the car to achieve.

Forward and back, reverse and drive, over and over Dusty repeated the procedure, but the Buick would not pull itself out. Sandy gritted her teeth and swayed with the movement as Dusty repeated the grim undertaking.

Finally, he stopped and poked his head out the window. "Maybe I can push it, if you'll drive," he said. "The ground got softer, and I can't get it out this way."

She nodded, walked through the mud, and climbed behind the steering wheel.

"I'll tell you when to go," he said, sliding from the slippery bank into the creek.

Slipping the control into the lowest gear, she waited for his signal and wiped her sweating palms on the steering wheel. When she heard Dusty's voice, she pushed on the foot feed.

"Gently now," Dusty shouted.

She felt herself pushing on the steering wheel and hoping that would help, but the tires only spun and whined in agony.

"Don't stop," Dusty ordered. "Gun it now."

She jammed the foot feed to the floor and joyously felt the car move forward. "Come on," she yelled at it. "You can do it. Come on. Come on."

The front wheel drive finally caught solid ground and Sandy felt it serge ahead down the road before she moved her foot to the brake. Blowing the air from her lungs, she didn't realize she'd been holding her breath. Glancing in the rear view mirror, she observed Dusty covered with mud from head to toe and wiping the slime from his face. She tried not to laugh, but the sight was too overwhelming, and she couldn't control her laughter.

"Think it's funny, do you?" Dusty said as he slumped onto the passenger seat. "Next time you can push."

Sandy laughed, forced the car into drive and headed for the cabin.

"Do you suppose we can take time to eat some of Grandma Lily's lunch?" she asked. "Hopefully it's still in the pickup."

"Let's just grab it and go," Dusty urged. "I can't get out of here soon enough."

"We have to go past the cabin, anyway, to get to the other road out. It should be drier although it's longer."

"Whatever," Dusty said. "Let's just do it."

Chapter 25

As Sandy stopped the car in front of the cabin, Dusty quickly jumped out, checked the pickup's bed, and held up the picnic basket, but as he opened the car door to set it in the front seat between them, movement at the cabin door caught his attention.

"I think we have company," he said, nodding toward the cabin.

Sandy spun her attention from the basket to the building's open door. "Sterling," she gasped. "How'd he get here?"

"I'd guess we didn't do a good enough job with our clubs and rocks," Dusty grunted.

"And he still has his gun," Sandy said disgustedly. "I think he wants us to come over there."

"Maybe we could make a run for it in the car," Dusty suggested as he watched Sterling approach. "How about running him over?"

She slammed the gear into reverse, but when bullets zinged through the windshield, she decided the smartest thing to do was to stop.

"You've found it, haven't you?" Sterling asked as he approached. "You've found the brooch."

"No, we haven't." Sandy felt her voice shaking. "We were just leaving. Do you want to join us?" She grumbled at herself. "Why'd I say that?" she whispered. Then smiling she eyed the picnic basket. Perhaps that would lure him to drop his guard. "We've some lunch here. Would you like some?"

Sterling licked his lips but motioned for them to get out of the car. "Not until I have that brooch in my hand."

Sandy studied the man's withering condition from the purple bruise on his head to his shaking hands and hoped his physical limitations would cause more vulnerability in the man. She watched him rub his head possibly to stay alert. Somehow she must sway him off his guard.

"I have no idea where it is," Sandy said as she stepped from the car. "We've looked and looked. It simply doesn't seem to be here."

"Then you'd better start thinking again," Sterling said waving the gun at Dusty. "I wouldn't want your cowboy to get hurt."

Although she tried to stay calm, Sandy's heart felt like it surged to her throat. She gazed at Dusty as a new plan seeped into her mind. "Okay, okay, she finally said. "It's probably buried beneath the pine tree by the stream. Grandpa put everything there." *Yes, especially all his garbage*, she thought. "We'll need a shovel."

"You find one," Sterling said. "The cowboy waits with me."

Sandy raced to the cabin where Dusty left the shovel, stopping only once to check the road for a police car. She clinched her fists in disgust and growled under her breath. "What could be taking the police so long?" She studied the road again then grabbed the shovel and gazed at the hammer on the table. With no place to hide it, she grasped the shovel as a club and swung it. The tool would make a fine weapon.

She strode slowly to the pine tree, her eyes fixed on the road. Surely they would arrive soon. She'd just have to dig slowly.

"It's probably right here," she said, letting the spade fall and cut into the pine needles beneath the tree.

"Go to it." Sterling sat below the branches and waved the gun at her. "Your friend can sit here beside me."

Sandy glared at him then shoved the shovel into the dirt pushing the tool with her foot. Spadefuls after spadefuls brought only the dark moist soil. Sandy wiped the perspiration from her forehead and slammed the shovel into the dirt again as the tool began to bring up old bottles and cans. Carefully she looked at each object, but as she knew, no brooch appeared.

"It may be in a box or something," she told Sterling. "I don't really know what to look for."

"The brooch has the biggest ruby you ever saw," Sterling said, leaning forward. "You'll know it when you see it."

Sandy watched him wipe at his hair then scoot away from the tree.

"Bloody tree," he growled. "Its sap is oozing out."

Sandy smiled and drove the spade into the hole again. The tree was still sappy. Sapplehead is a good name. She stopped momentarily and gazed at the tree and smiled at the pleasant memories filling her mind. Grandpa sat against that tree many years ago. She shook her head as she stopped to catch her breath. The tree or something related to the sap incident might just be the clue. Her mind buzzed with events surrounding the sap and the tree. She resumed digging and as the shovel struck a glass jar and broke it, she searched the hole. It contained nothing but junk. The only other event worth considering would be fishing. Something to do with fishing could be the clue to the brooch's location.

She leaned on the shovel and gazed at the clear rushing stream. The brooch would be washed away in the water unless Grandpa anchored it with something.

Sterling brought her attention back to digging. "You haven't dug far enough to give up now," he said.

Sandy rubbed her back. "Could Dusty dig awhile?" She stepped from the hole and handed the shovel to Dusty. Sterling seemed unmoved by the change in diggers and Sandy noticed his head nodding forward. She sat down beneath the pine and the steady clump, clump of the shovel dulled her mind, and she shook her head to keep from dozing.

She studied Sterling nodding at the rhythmic sound of the shovel. Now would be the time to overpower him, but her mind felt fuzzy, and she could not persuade her body to move toward him. In the numb world of half sleep, Sandy thought the shovel stopped and she shook the drowsiness from her mind as her gaze moved from Dusty leaning on the shovel to a sound coming from the far side of the meadow. She quickly rose as a vehicle's motor rumbled clearly in the clean, sharp air.

The thrill of rescue flashed through her when she saw a Jeep on the old trail. It stopped at the edge of the meadow and two men inside gazed at the woman waving frantically at them.

Sandy flashed a glance at Sterling, her arms still above her head trying to gain the Jeep's attention as Sterling rose from his seat beside the tree and pointed his gun at Dusty. Sandy lowered her arms gazing at the Jeep parked at the edge of the meadow then at Sterling. Anger built up inside her and discouragement pushed the hope from her mind. Sterling would kill the men in the Jeep. They would, unknowingly, step into his deadly trap.

She wished she had not tried so hard to gain their attention. Her legs grew weak watching the Jeep bump toward her. Flinging her arms, she motioned for them to return the way they came but dropped her arms realizing the four wheel drive intended to stop and she could do nothing about it. At least she might be able to give them a message. Perhaps they would leave their fishing to go back to Centennial and phone the police.

All thoughts for rescue fled when Sandy watched Sterling walk toward the cabin pushing Dusty ahead of him, Sterling's gun in Dusty's back.

The Jeep stopped beside Sandy and a smiling face emerged from the window. "Is everything alright here? You waved like you needed some help."

Sandy fumbled for words. Her gaze flashed from Sterling back to the men in the Jeep. Reluctantly she shook her head. "No," she finally said. "Just waving. We've been here for a few days fishing. It's Just good to see a new face." She chuckled nervously.

"Catching anything?" the man asked. "We've used your cabin in the past. Hope you didn't mind."

Sandy glanced at the cabin, its interior in disarray. "Oh, no." She stared at Sterling then smiled at the Jeep's driver. "We'll be gone soon. Perhaps you could come back later." She hoped her words would not cause Sterling to do anything rash, but the gunman only glared at her.

"That's all right," the driver said. "We brought our tent just in case the cabin was being used."

A beam of hope danced into Sandy's mind. "Do many people use the cabin?"

"On weekends. We usually come up early to make sure we get the cabin."

Sandy silently recalled the days past. It's Saturday. There'll be others coming for the weekend. Excitement flashed through her. "Then you saw others on the road?"

"Not yet. We got an early start," the man said.

"No one else on the road?" Sandy asked, hoping he was mistaken.

The driver looked back down the trail then to Sandy. "You expecting someone?" He studied her worried eyes then pointed at Sterling. "Is that guy alright?"

Sandy flashed a look at Sterling's wounded head. "He fell on a rock. Yes, he's okay. We sent someone for some first-aid stuff. He'll be okay." She felt herself rambling and knew Sterling would soon make a move if she didn't discourage their staying. "Well, we'd better get to fishing if we're going to have any for supper."

The driver nodded and his eyes narrowed. "We'll be just upstream, there, if you need anything."

Sandy nodded, watching him eye Sterling cautiously. She sighed in relief when the driver sped back across the meadow.

Sterling stepped from behind Dusty, and Sandy noticed his gun shook in his hand.

"You just as well have told them to send the law," Sterling said. "Now, where is that brooch? You'd better find it before the next group comes."

Sandy's mind buzzed with fear. How could she find the brooch before the arrival of the next campers? Time seemed to have run out for them. Before the next car came across the meadow she had to have the brooch in her hand. Their only hope seemed to be the fishermen upstream and either she or Dusty had to somehow find their campsite. Obviously the police were not coming. She and Dusty had to handle the situation themselves. They needed another plan. She must persuade Sterling she suddenly remembered the gem's location and draw his attention away from Dusty. And she had to do it quickly.

Chapter 26

Sandy's breath came in gasps and her heart felt like the wings of a hummingbird. Her mind flashed with ideas where the brooch might be. Sapplehead. What did the word mean? Only the recollection of fishing resurfaced from the files of her memory. She studied the tree where her grandfather sat. Yes, she had been fishing that day. She shook her head to loosen any other memories of Sapplehead. Nothing came. The rushing creek must be the secret.

"The stream," she told Sterling. "It has to be in or along the water."

Sterling grinned and shook his head. "The river? I would have drifted away by now."

"Then where do you suggest, the outhouse? She glared at him and stomped toward the stream.

Sterling gave Dusty a push and forced him toward the rushing cold water.

Sandy studied the river's edge then walked along the bank. The pink wild roses rubbed her trousers sending their delicate blossoms sailing into the water like tiny velvet boats. Sandy watched them float until they stopped against the large stone at the edge of the water. The river bed formed a small eddy and the pink boats sailed around in a circle and docked against a sandy bar.

She knelt down beside a rock, half in and half out of the water and noticing a small hole beneath the stone, she embarked on a plan.

"There's a hole, here, under this rock," she called to Sterling.

Sterling's pace quickened as he ran toward Sandy's location leaving Dusty gazing after him.

"Here," Sandy said. "Below this rock. See? It looks like it's been chiseled out." Her gaze flashed past Sterling, kneeling to look at the hole, to Dusty racing into the trees down the river bank. She smiled and brought her attention back to Sterling.

"Don't you think it looks chiseled?" she asked.

Sterling rose to his feet and gazed at the hopeful expression on Sandy's face. "Could be," he said. He turned, searching behind for Dusty. The young man was nowhere in sight. "Well, you'll have to do this alone," Sterling said. "Dig in and see what you find."

Sandy dropped to her knees and pulled at the sand in the hole. She worked slowly giving Dusty time to get to the fishermen. Knowing Sterling would soon become discouraged at this location, Sandy's mind buzzed thinking of another site. She reached far into the hole and was surprised as she pulled out a rusty tobacco tin. The narrow, once red, can would fit into a man's shirt pocket.

Sandy gazed at the cannot believing her eyes. This didn't make sense. Grandfather's note had nothing to do with sap or fishing or anything like that.

Sterling grabbed the can from her and held it close to his chest. His eyes shone and a satisfied chuckle escaped from his throat. "I'll have it all myself," he gloated.

He stuck the gun in the belt of his trousers and pulled his handkerchief from his pocket. Gently he wrapped it around the rusty tin then slowly placed the bundle in his suit pocket.

"Aren't you even going to look at it?" Sandy asked. She would have liked to have seen the cause of all she had been through.

Sterling patted the pocket. "I know it's there. Now there's only one duty left to do.

Sandy's heart skipped a beat when he reached for his gun. Her gaze flashed to the woods on the far side of the stream. Too far to run.

She needed a diversion. She looked toward the cabin and shook her finger in that direction. Her heart quickened its beating and she felt her raised arm shaking. "There's another car coming," she warned him as she pointed toward the cabin.

Sterling's back ward glance was part of the watchfulness of the man. Whether he believed her or not had nothing to do with the automatic motion.

The look took only a second but gave Sandy the time she needed to kick the gun. The blow caused Sterling to drop the weapon, but before Sandy could get to the middle of the stream, he had the gun in his hand again.

"Stop right there, little lady," Sterling screamed at her.

Sandy stopped and turned to face him. "Okay, okay," she said, sighing as if it were her last breath. "You have the brooch. You'd better get out before somebody really comes." Her mind fought for ideas to prolong Sterling's plan until Dusty came with help. "If those fishermen see what you're doing, you'll die for sure. They had rifles in their Jeep."

Sandy planned while the words spilled from her mouth. She squealed and faltered on the stream's slippery rocks as if to fall. Landing on her knees in the water, she quickly grabbed a stone in each hand. Flinging them at the gunman, she didn't wait for his reaction, but fled to the far side of the stream.

Her heart drummed inside her shirt as she watched Sterling bound into the stream after her. She raced through the sunlight that pierced the forest carpet and left dark shadows behind the stones. Sandy chanced a look over her shoulder and saw Sterling trip over a tree root extending above the ground. She stopped behind a large rock gasping for breath. Hearing the rushing stream, she decided she must be running parallel to it. If she could cross without Sterling seeing her, he may be confused enough to give up the chase and leave with the brooch. Darting from behind the rock a thought flashed through her mind. Something Dusty said about Sterling being such a good tracker. Too late now. The stream rushed before her.

She stumbled into the icy water and groaned as her boot slipped on the stones in the creek's bed. Her eyes grew wide, and she gasped as the stream surged around her. She fought for footing, flinging her hands, and kicking. The current pulled her downstream until she hit a stone sticking out of the water. She grabbed the stone and shook the water from her eyes. On one bank Sterling stood laughing at her. On the other she saw the cabin. The current brought her back where she started her run for life. Quickly she slipped behind the stone keeping it between her and Sterling.

"You can't stay there all night," Sterling shouted over the water's rushing. "You might as well come out and take it like a man."

Take it like a man? But she was a woman and would not stand and take it. She felt her feet becoming numb in the cold water. It hurt her skin as if it were burning. Perhaps Sterling wasn't accurate at hitting a running target. It seemed Dusty said that at one time or another. She reached into the water and rubbed her legs. How could she move being so cold? Oh, where was Dusty?

She gazed over her shoulder toward the cabin. All seemed much too still. Nothing moved. Not a Jeep or patrol car. Her cold hands suddenly slipped from the rock and Sandy felt herself being pulled by the water. A shot rang out and hit beside her in the stream making a little splat sound.

Quickly she tossed and turned in the water hoping his target moved fast enough to be missed. She heard him laughing and hot anger flooded her body. Rising to her feet, she saw him bending over with laughter. She growled with anger and started picking up stones and throwing them as hard as she could. The man only laughed as the stones pelted him. "He's enjoying this," she whispered. "And he wants it to last a good long time." Like a cornered mouse, she waded to the river's edge and saw him step into the stream.

"Run where you will," Sterling called amid his laughter. "You can't get away from me."

Sandy shook with cold and fear realizing he was right. Her only alternative seemed to be to stand and fight. She gazed desperately toward the road hoping to see a car coming down the trail. Other fishermen must have decided against venturing to the cabin this weekend. Her gaze darted to the cabin and her mind surveyed its interior for a weapon. Only sticks and stones were left for her.

She turned to face Sterling. The grinning man stepped from the water and slowly walked toward her. Then something else caught her attention on the other side of the stream. Dusty. Sandy's heart thumped at the sight of the young man sneaking from tree to tree. Keeping Sterling's attention from him, Sandy started for the cabin. Sterling followed chuckling as he strode.

"Yes," Sterling told her. "The cabin would be nice, too. I don't believe there's a weapon in there, though."

Sandy darted behind the house and pushed on the bedroom windows but couldn't force them open. She had to keep Sterling from seeing Dusty as he crossed the stream. If she could just persuade Sterling to follow her behind the cabin it would give Dusty enough time to get across the water. She flattened herself against the wall and waited. When Sterling didn't appear, she ventured a glance around the building.

She gasped seeing Dusty running toward Sterling. On the open meadow Sterling could turn and fire before Dusty could get to him. She yelled at Sterling and the grinning man took a few steps toward her then stopped. He glanced behind him, but Dusty stepped behind the outhouse.

"I was just going to tell you there's someone behind you," she said boldly.

Sterling gazed at her, and his grin dropped to a frown as he spun to view the river behind him.

Sandy sped around the cabin and hopped through the cabin's open door. Quickly she closed it behind her, picked up a table leg and waited beside the door. Her hand shook as she listened for footsteps outside and watched for the doorknob to turn. Her wet clothes and the tension of waiting sent a shiver through her, and she felt her teeth chattering.

The wet clothes clung to her, and she gazed at the wool blanket in the bedroom then back to the closed door. Slowly lowering the table's leg Sandy raced for the blanket and wrapped it around her trembling shoulders. Taking her place beside the door, she raised the wooden weapon once more.

Her arms ached with the waiting. Sterling surely realized where she'd hidden. Why wasn't he coming? Silence drummed in her ears. An eerie heavy stillness, as before the first peal of thunder in an approaching storm, filled the air. Sandy felt her teeth grinding. The sound seemed to echo through the silent cabin. Her tense muscles screamed to relax.

Then, as if in slow motion, Sandy's gaze snapped to the small windows above the couch. The glass shattered spraying the room with tiny, sharp spears. Sandy forced herself against the wall when she saw Sterling's gun poke through the opening. A gasp escaped from her throat and her eyes widened with fear. She stood pinned against the wall unable to move. Anger filled her when Sterling pulled the weapon from the window and laughed.

"You must do better than that," he said. "I'll give you one more chance to run for your life."

Sandy heard his laughter from the window then the man seemed to grunt and groan. She rushed to the window and saw Dusty jump him from behind and had his arm around Sterling's neck demanding he drop the gun.

Sandy ran from the cabin wrapped like a Native American woman in the blanket. Rounding the corner, she saw Sterling fighting savagely to fling Dusty from his back. She watched Dusty fly over Sterling's head and land with a groan on the ground. The gun still in his hand, Sterling pointed it toward Dusty lying on the meadow grass.

A growl rose from Sandy's throat. She flung the blanket off her shoulders and covered Sterling's head with its wooly surface. Jumping onto the man she forced him to the ground. From outside the blanket, she beat on her assailant wishing she brought the table leg.

Dusty jumped up and helped her when Sterling fought to free himself from the wooly prison. Finally, Sterling lay still, and Sandy backed away from the woolen lump.

"I thought you were going for help," she told Dusty. Her voice shook and her wet, chilled body trembled.

Dusty stepped toward her and held her close. "I couldn't leave you alone with him."

She nodded close to his chest. "I'm glad you came back."

Dusty stepped from her and pulled the blanket off Sterling. He intended wrapping it around Sandy, but Sterling, waiting for such a move, raised the gun and fired. Dusty crumbled and fell at Sandy's feet.

Rage filled Sandy and she rushed at Sterling knocking him off balance. He flung her aside and she landed on the ground beside Dusty. She glared at Sterling then laid her hand on the young blond man and wept.

Sterling pulled her from Dusty's side to her feet. "Now, I'll give you a head start," he said squeezing her arm then pushing her away.

Sandy gazed at Dusty's still form then at the trees beside the stream. The pine her grandfather sat against loomed before her. He may let her get that far just for the sport of the chase.

She ran wildly toward the tree beside the stream and hurled herself behind it. She peered around it at Sterling coming slowly and confidently. Frantically she picked up a stone and waited. Tears came to her eyes as she remembered what Dusty always said. Yes, more sticks and stones.

"You tired running?" Sterling asked, stopping at the tree.

With all the force she had, Sandy hurled the stone at him. Her eyes brightened seeing the stone hit the gun, sending it to the ground.

Sterling scrambled for the weapon, but Sandy jumped onto him and pulled him away from his intended goal. She hit him with her fists and kicked him, but the man pulled her off as one would a wood tick and flung her against the tree.

Sandy fought for her breath that the tree knocked from her and watched Sterling scramble on hands and knees toward the gun. Quickly she searched the ground for a weapon. No time to hide, she picked up a branch that had fallen from the ancient tree, but lifting it, realized the movement futile. Sterling had the gun.

"This looks like a good a place as any," he said, smiling broadly. "I'll put you out of your misery."

Sandy backed against the tree. Was this where it all ends against the Sapplehead tree? The Sapplehead tree. Her mind dashed scenes of Grandpa sitting here and the sap on his head. The sap. An unanswered question went through her mind. What did sap have to do with the tobacco tin Sterling had in his pocket? She took a deep breath and met Sterling's gaze.

"Could I see the brooch before -?" She swallowed at the familiar lump in her throat, her eyes pleading for this last request.

Sterling slowly pulled the tin from his pocket. "This is not leaving my person until I'm safely back in England."

Sandy's glance slid from his face to Dusty, slowly raising to his feet and staggering toward Sterling. Her heart leaped as she quickly moved her gaze back to Sterling. She must keep the gunman from turning and seeing Dusty creeping up behind him.

"The clue has nothing to do with a tobacco can," Sandy said, trying to keep Sterling's attention on her. "It has to do with sap. And the only sap is in the tree."

Sterling's smile dropped to a frown momentarily then he shook his head, an evil grin spreading across his face. "It's not going to work this time. You're just buying time, waiting for someone to come up that road." As his gaze moved from her to the road, the image of Dusty caught in his field of vision. He turned quickly to face the wounded man standing behind him.

Dusty stopped, seeing the gun pointed his way and pulled himself beside Sandy who stood against the tree.

Sandy closed her eyes waiting for Sterling to pull the trigger.

Chapter 27

Sandy's father, Bradly and Tom led the police car down the highway but turned onto a gravel road before reaching Centennial. Tom sped along faster than usual for the long way to the cabin took more than an hour. The police car lagged behind trying to avoid the gravel flying from Tom's tires.

The gravel road turned and twisted over the flat Laramie Basin ending at the edge of the tall pines standing guard over the high country. There it became a Jeep trail climbing skyward with rocks jutting from its mountain soil and ruts deepened by years of travel.

Tom stopped at the edge of the timber waiting for the cruiser to catch up. "I hope nothing's happened up there." He nodded in the direction of the cabin.

"Me, too," Bradly said. "We'd had an earlier start if those cops wouldn't have had to call in every minute." He checked his watch. "Ten thirty already. A lot could have happened between the time Sandy left and now." He looked out the rear window.

"Are they coming?" Tom asked.

"Oh, the cops? Yes." Bradly craned his neck to search the sky.

"Are you expecting eagles?" Tom asked as he gazed out the driver's window.

"In some sense of the word," Bradly chuckled. "I called for a helicopter."

"Oh, ho," Tom said and patted the steering wheel. "And you think they'll come? Sounds like a long shot to me."

Bradly sighed and shook his head. "Yeah, it does, but I had to try everything and everyone I knew."

"Who knows?" Tom shrugged. "Maybe we'll get lucky."

"Here's the cruiser now. I'll talk to them a bit. Worn them about what to expect on this road." Bradly said and stepped from the pickup. When he returned, he nodded toward the road. "They've been up here before. Of course, not in a cruiser so it looks like we're all set."

"Okay," Tom said. "I hope the only ones there are Sandy and Dusty eating Lily's lunch and doing what young people do."

Bradly laughed. "Sandy has a lot of common sense." He stopped laughing and frowned. "Yet, she's still a young girl"

"Oh, she'll be alright," Tom reassured him. "She nothing to fear from Dusty. It's others up there I'm worried about."

"Yeah," Bradly agreed. "I just hope they weren't followed."

The road twisted upward, and Tom slowed his pace to keep the police car in sight. He could almost hear the rocks scraping the bottom of the cruiser.

"Not really a good road for them," Tom told Bradly.

"Well, we're almost to the top. Now the road will wind around north then west. We'll come in on the west side of the cabin."

When the cruiser finished the climb, Bradly noticed the long scrape on the side reaching from the front fender to the rear.

"Looks like he got too close to the rocks," he chuckled. "Gashed that car up good."

"It'll be easier from now on. Rocks will be the least of their troubles," Tom said as he headed the four wheel drive down the first hill.

The trail curved and bumped among the pines and was rocky and dry on the higher portions, but at the bottom the road ran across small streams of melted snow running from the higher elevations.

Tom stopped after passing through each muddy stretch and waited for the car to grind through. "Maybe we should have them jump in the back of the pickup. We'd make better time," he said.

"Just go," Bradly said. "We're wasting time talking."

"Onward and upward and downward," Tom said as he checked the rear view mirror for the police car. "Looks like he's having trouble on that little muddy streak," he said as he observed the cruiser fish tail and spin then grab solid ground. "I'll bet we have to pull him out pretty soon."

"Don't ask for trouble," Bradly said. "We probably have enough of that."

The next depression didn't appear any different from the last, but the soft earth extended farther. Tom gunned the pickup and it ground its way across the soggy grass. The cruiser didn't fair as well as it bogged down half way across the moist bottomland.

"I guess we'd better try out that new winch," Bradly said as he stepped from the pickup.

"Just toss the end of the cord," the officer shouted from the car. "I'll attach it on. You don't have to get in the mud."

"Good enough," Bradly said as he threw the cord with the hook on the end. "I hope this thing works," he told Tom.

"Oh, yeah," Tom said confidently. "I've been practicing."

"You would," Bradly chuckled. "Okay, let's see how she works."

Tom slid into the pickup and simply pushed a button, and the machine began grinding and pulling the cruiser from the mud.

"Now that is what I call a gem," Bradly said as the patrol car sat on solid ground. "I got to get me one of those." As he slid onto the passenger seat beside Tom, Bradly's tone became more serious. "Now let's see what those two kids got themselves into."

The trail climbed higher as they proceeded leaving the marshy lowlands behind. Pines hugged the road as the forest became denser and a sharp coolness permeated the air. Bradly squirmed in his seat as he studied the terrain.

"It's not too far now," he said. "Anyway, there shouldn't be any more mud holes. Just around this hill and we turn east. The cabin's not far once we round this bend."

Tom nodded then squinted as he gazed through the windshield. "Who in the world is that? Looks like some guy staggering down the road. He must be drunk. Look at him."

Bradly stared at the rather heavy set man trying to stay on his feet as he hurried toward them.

"We'd better stop and give him a hand," Bradly said as he grabbed the door handle. "I don't think he'll make another step." As Bradly stepped out, the man stopped then turned and tried to run, but fell on the forest road. Bradly and Tom pulled him to his feet as the officers ran to assist them.

"Take it easy fella," Bradly said. "We're here to help you." He let the man lean against him. "What are you doing way out here alone? It looks like you ran into a bear or something."

"Something like that," the man said.

His British accent stunned Bradly for a moment. He gazed at the man then studied the road to the cabin. "What are you doing up here?"

"Just walking. Trying to find a way out of these bloody woods," the man said with a weak chuckle.

"What happened to you?" Tom asked. "Was it a bear or a big cat?"

"Somewhat a bit of both," the man said. "Actually, it was my partner. We had a disagreement."

"Looks like a big one," Bradly said studying the bruises on the man's face. "By the way, I'm Bradly and this is Tom. What's your name?"

"I'm Livingstone. Livingstone Brownly.

Bradly swallowed hard and felt his teeth grinding as anger surged from his chest, but he tried to control his rage. "I'm Bradly Templeton.

My cabin is just around the bend. We can take you there and you can rest."

"Oh, no," Livingstone screamed. "I can't go back there. Sterling will kill me for sure. Just take me away."

"We'll take you away alright," Tom said. "What's going on up there with Sandy and Dusty?"

Livingstone wilted and Bradly pulled him to his feet. "Tell me what's going on at the cabin?"

"I'd say you'd better get up there as quickly as you can. Sterling has those young people searching for that brooch. I'm afraid he's going to try and kill them, too. He's gone crazy."

"Let's put him in the patrol car," Bradly said. "And get to that cabin." He studied the sky as he heard a steady put, put of a helicopter approaching from the east. "We've really got assistance now. Let's get that guy."

Chapter 28

Sandy raised her hands and covered her face. She felt Dusty slip to the ground. There had been no blast from Sterling's gun. Had she not heard it? The only sound filling the cool, clean air was a loud click, then another. She opened her eyes realizing Sterling's gun clicked against an empty cylinder. Her next thought flashed to the branch lying beside the tree. A growl, low and angry, brought her attention back to Sterling.

He stood red faced, his fists clinched at his sides. The empty gun dropped from his hand, and he rushed at Sandy. "You can't get away even without the gun," he yelled.

Sandy stepped away from the angry rush letting Sterling hit the tree with the full impact of his anger. She reached for the branch, but Sterling grabbed her arm. Sandy squealed at his tight hold, gasping as he tried to pull her from her feet. A quick kick freed her arm and she raced from the tree toward the stream.

Glancing over her shoulder, she saw Sterling on her heels. She tried to turn from his grasping hands but felt his tight hold on her shoulder. She wiggled and squirmed to loosen his hold.

Sterling smiled at her fighting, turned her around and pushed her into the stream.

Sandy pushed at the water flowing over her face then gasped at Sterling standing above her holding a large rock over his head.

"Now," he said. "Finally, an end to you."

Sandy splashed quickly from under the path of the stone, and it fell heavily missing its target.

Sterling, annoyed by another failure, rushed at her, trying to pull her into the deeper water in the stream.

Sandy, seeing his arms reaching out for her, slipped from his path. She forced herself toward the bank, her breath coming in short frightened gasps. Then the slippery rocks in the stream's bed sent her legs from under her.

Sterling stood above her once again, his gaze searching for another large stone. His attention drawn from her, Sandy grabbed his legs and pulled them with all her strength.

Sterling fell, yelling, into the cold water. He tried to get to his feet but slipped on the stones. He lay only a moment watching Sandy scramble onto the bank.

Sandy turned toward him, pelting him with the stones from the river bank. When she saw those didn't stop him, her thoughts turned toward the cabin and the sturdy table legs or the shovel. Where did she leave the shovel? Beside the tree where they dug the hole.

She watched Sterling splash from the stream and decided the table leg would be better. Leading him back to the cabin would possibly protect Dusty lying beside the pine tree. Racing to the cabin, Sandy glanced over her shoulder to see how close Sterling ran behind her. The meadow, behind her, seemed empty. She stopped and flashed a glance to the left and right. The man could not have possibly gotten to the cabin first.

Her gaze stopped at the pine beside the stream. Sterling stopped beneath the tree searching for something. The gun. He'll load the gun before coming after her. She grumbled in disgust at not running for the shovel. At least she may have prevented him from loading the gun.

Stomping into the cabin, she angrily picked up a table leg. Grabbing it tightly, she waited by the door. When no one bounded through, Sandy slowly stepped to the window and peered out. Only the empty meadow met her gaze. Where could he be? Her glance moved back to the door then settled on the bedroom. She wiped her palms on her slacks and stepped silently toward the bedroom, the table leg held above her head ready to strike.

Sticks against a gun? Her mind heard Dusty ask. He always worried about her primitive methods against Sterling's weapons. She had no choice. If Sterling waited in the bedroom, she would do her best with the club until he brought her down.

Sandy took a deep breath and hesitated beside the bedroom entrance then stepped in hurling the leg against the wall where Sterling could be standing. She sighed at the emptiness of the room. Her gaze fell on the windows hoping Sterling was too big to enter.

All her attention flashed to the front door. Sterling with his gun had to be there now. Slipping behind the door she waited. Perspiration mingled with the river water trickled down her forehead. It tickled her nose, but she tried to ignore it, her hands being occupied with the club above her head. She listened. No sound came from the kitchen. Turning, she peered through the crack where the door's hinges left a space. Nothing appeared in the small opening.

She resumed her position holding tightly to the table leg, ready to swing it at the footsteps approaching. She felt him standing in the doorway.

"Sandy?" the voice from the door belonged to Dusty.

Sandy lowered the club with shaking hands and rushed to him. She caught him as he slumped toward the floor.

"He came back for the gun," Dusty said. "But I hid it."

Sandy helped him to the slashed mattress and checked the wound in his shoulder. "It looks bad to me," she said. "We need help." She checked the front door. "Where is Sterling?"

"I got him with a branch. He's not done for, but you'll have time to get out of here."

"Alone?" Her eyes grew wide, and a flash of anger spread through her. "I'm not leaving you here. He'll find the gun and come looking for us."

"There's a hole in the tree, partially grown over, but the gun fit in with a little pushing. He won't find it," Dusty said then groaned at the pain.

A hole in the tree. Sandy gazed toward the window. Could Sterling be mistaken about the tobacco can? Sapplehead. Sap. Those clues certainly had nothing to do with a tobacco can.

"What kind of hole?" she asked.

"Just a hole. Probably a squirrel or something made it. Only a little opening left. The tree is covering it up. Healing its own wound." He pushed at his wounded shoulder. "Wish I could."

"We have to get out of here," she said as she frantically gazed around the room then stopped and rushed to the door. "Sterling's car. It's right outside." She hurried back to him. "I forget about Sterling's car. The keys must still be in it." She felt her heart pounding with relief. "Come on. I'll help you. We can get away in Sterling's car."

"No, no," he said weakly. "Sterling took them before we went to that pine tree to dig that worthless hole."

"Oh, no, not again." Sandy sat on the bed beside him and sighed. "Then there's only one thing left to do. I have to find those fishermen."

"I can't go with you," he said, trying to smile. "I don't think I can make it." He drew a deep breath. "How about those police? Shouldn't be here by now?"

"I don't think they're coming," she said, shaking her head. "We're on our own."

She rubbed his hand, bent over, and kissed him. "All right. I'll be back as soon as I can."

As she left him on the bed and raced from the cabin, movement under the Sapplehead tree caught her attention. Sterling staggered to his feet, his angry gaze falling upon her. She watched him pick up the branch Dusty had used on him. The only thought racing through her mind centered on keeping Sterling from going to the cabin. Dusty's weakened condition would not enable him to fight with Sterling.

Leading the gunman into the timber seemed her only alternative. Perhaps his tracking skills were dulled by the blows to his head. Maybe she could lead him toward the fishermen and they, the two young strong men, could overpower her assailant.

She forced her tired, frightened body across the stream and fled among the trees. Shadows hid her escape, and she ignored the coolness carried on the west wind. She stopped behind a tree and gazed through the shade cast by the forest. The breaking twigs told her that Sterling followed closely. He ceased his usual silent carefulness and surged blindly through the timber. She felt certain he followed her appearing and disappearing in the shadowed, silent temple of pines.

Sandy scrambled over a fallen tree and headed back toward the stream where she hoped to find the fishermen. Realizing she couldn't lose Sterling in the timber, she quickened her pace through the shadows. At the water's edge, she stopped and gazed at the tree's crowns. Daylight danced in the tops of the trees, but there was something else. An odd sound that didn't belong to this world of birds and bees and whispering pines. She shook her head knowing her exhaustion was having an effect on her hearing.

"Okay, just upstream," she said. "Or did the fishermen say downstream?" She couldn't remember now. Fear rushed into her mind. Could she be going in the wrong direction? She thought of Dusty in the bed at the cabin. He might die without help. She took a deep breath and started upstream.

Nothing could be seen of the fishermen. Sandy stopped again and looked behind her. Even Sterling must have given up this time. A soft hum in the tree tops filled the forest and mingled with a putting sound she couldn't distinguish.

She sighed knowing Sterling didn't give up easily. Although she couldn't see him a feeling told her of his close presence. Crossing the water might slow his assault. She plunged into the water gasping at its coldness and fought the current to the other side. Her startled gaze met Sterling's

The man had crossed downstream, seeming to sense her thoughts. Yes, his tracking abilities were exceptional. A sound moved her attention further upstream. Men laughing. The fishermen. She gazed back at Sterling then dashed toward the sound, screaming to attract attention.

"Hello," she yelled. "Help. I'm the woman from the cabin. I need your help."

Sterling tackled her and brought her to the ground. She groaned and kicked at him, flinging her fists at the man who worked his way to her throat.

"Those men are far away," Sterling told her. "Sound carries very well in the woods. By the time they get here you'll be dead, and I'll be gone."

Sandy pushed at him with one hand and with the other searched for something to defend herself. The free hand found a stone and Sandy raised it as Sterling tightened his hold around her throat. The stone landed with a glancing blow on the side of Sterling's head and the man reeled and loosened his hold on her.

Sandy pushed the groggy man from her and quickly got to her feet. She backed away from the man, her gaze upstream. Sterling moved quickly and barred her way from the fisherman's campsite. She turned and ran wildly back the way she came, toward the cabin.

Tossing all caution aside, she hopped the fallen trees and, without looking back, surged through the forest. She heard men's voices calling to her. The fishermen heard her, but she had no breath to call back. What little she felt heaving in her chest caught in tiny sobs and she fought back tears that made the forest appear to be submerged in water.

Before her the cabin stood in the bright sunlight so peaceful in the midst of her panic. She stopped at the Sapplehead tree unable to go further. Her lungs felt as though they would explode, and her legs trembled. She stopped behind the tree knowing she couldn't hide from Sterling but realized she must make a stand. Lifting the branch from the needled carpet, she waited for him. She pulled the cool air into her lungs and urged all her strength toward the branch in her hands.

The men shouting flooded the forest. She wanted to call back then realized it would make no difference. Sterling knew where she stood, anyway. She took a deep breath and stepped from behind the tree.

"I'm here," she shouted as loudly as she could. "Near the cabin. Hurry."

Sterling stepped from the shadows and grabbed her hand holding the branch. His gaze caught the handle of his gun sticking from the hole in the tree. He gave Sandy a shove and pulled the weapon from the hole.

Sandy landed beside the depression she and Dusty dug searching for the brooch. She watched Sterling quickly pull a clip of bullets from his jacket pocket. Her gaze darted to the ground for the fallen branch for now he would not only shoot her, but also the fishermen crashing through the underbrush.

She grabbed the branch then both she and Sterling stopped still. From above, a loud thumping sound filled the forest. The same sound she heard earlier. A helicopter landing in the meadow beside the cabin made Sandy's heart leap. And down the road Tom's pickup bumped ahead of a patrol car, its siren screaming.

"They're here, Sterling. You just as well give up." Sandy stood, branch in hand, watching him trying to jam the clip into the gun.

"That's okay," he said, grinning at her. "You'll not live to see it happen." He fought with the clip, forcing it toward its place in the gun.

Sandy looked at the helicopter then at the pickup and patrol car stopping at the cabin. Through the forest she could see the hats of the fishermen bobbing as the men approaching jumped the fallen logs. She realized Sterling wouldn't allow more time for talk. He assumed the position of a cornered mountain cat.

Unable to force the clip into the gun, Sterling tossed it aside as his face filled with desperation. He growled as Sandy swung the branch and he caught it in mid-flight.

Sandy stepped back as he threw the branch aside. She moved slowly around the tree hoping for a chance to push him toward the hole she had dug, chanced a glance at the cabin and saw her father and Tom enter the log structure. Dusty would be alright now, but it seemed too late for her. She gasped as Sterling dashed angrily toward her.

Chapter 29

Sandy tried to sidestep Sterling's onrush, but he caught her arm and pulled her toward him.

"The rescue mission won't do you any good," he said, snarling behind his teeth.

Sandy lowered her chin when Sterling's arm moved to encircle her throat. She knew he was enjoying this and pushed at his elbow approaching her chin and sank her teeth into his arm.

Sterling quickly unwrapped his hold on her, shook his arm and reached for her again.

Sandy slipped away from his reaching arms, her gaze on the cabin. If she could run to the cabin, she'd be safe. She dashed around the tree then stopped short. In front of her loomed the freshly dug hole. Trying to miss it, Sandy jumped to its side, her ankle twisting when she landed off balance. She rose quickly and forced her foot to accept her weight. Glancing at Sterling, she noticed him working with the gun, pulling out the empty clip. Gritting her teeth in anger, she rushed toward him. If he slipped the full clip into the gun, she would have no chance getting to the cabin.

The clip, full of bullets, fell from his hand when Sandy jumped onto Sterling. He scrambled for it, Sandy clinging to his back, pulling his hair and kicking him.

Sandy forced him to the ground, both reaching for the loaded clip. With all her strength, Sandy pulled him from his goal, but he yanked his arm from her hold and his hand landed on the clip.

Sandy's breathe came in frightened gasps. She picked up a stone and smashed the hand grasping the clip of bullets. She grabbed the clip when Sterling released it and rising quickly, she threw the clip into the forest.

Once again she gazed at the cabin and saw her father leading a policeman toward her. She smiled with relief and started to run to them. "I'm here," she called.

Sterling grabbed the injured ankle and brought her to the ground. Sandy cringed at the pain but kicked herself free and scrambled around the tree. She held her breath as Sterling looked at the men approaching across the meadow then he lunged at her. Gasping, Sandy started to limp toward the forest behind her and the fishermen crashing toward her. She stopped short when Sterling yelled. A deadly silence followed.

Sandy waited, her back to Sterling. She waited in the cool June silence for his hands to grab her throat. When no attack came, she turned toward the Sapplehead tree.

Sterling lay at the foot of the towering pine, his head, face down, resting against a stone protruding from the meadow's grassy floor.

Sandy stood fighting back tears of relief. Through a veil of moisture, she watched her father and the patrolman turn Sterling over, his unseeing eyes gazing at the swaying branches of the Sapplehead tree. She approached him slowly; unsure Sterling would not rise up to attack again.

"He's done for," the patrolman said. "It looks like he tripped on the root of this tree and hit his head on the rock."

Sandy sobbed with relief. The Sapplehead tree had gotten him, as if it reached out and grabbed his foot then slammed him against the stone.

The patrolman searched Sterling's pockets and brought out the keys to Bradly's pickup, the car keys and the rusty tobacco tin carefully wrapped in the handkerchief.

"I'd like to see that," Sandy said, reaching for the can.

She slowly unwrapped the tin, opened the rusted lid and dropped its contents into her hand. Three of Grandpa's favorite fishing lures fell from the can. Looking at the lures, she smiled at Sterling's staring eyes.

"Just fishing lures, Sterling," she said. "You died for fishing lures."

The sound of the helicopter taking off pulled her attention from Sterling's still form. "Is the helicopter leaving already?" she asked.

"Yes. It's taking that wounded fellow to the hospital," he said.

Dusty. She dropped the tin and lures and hurriedly limped onto the meadow waving her hands for the whirling blades to stop. She hadn't even said good-bye. An empty feeling engulfed her as the helicopter rose above her and disappeared above the trees. She watched it through a glaze of tears.

"Dusty," she called. "Oh, Dusty." She waved again then fell to her knees in the meadow. Listening to the put, put of the engine growing fainter, she clasped her chest as the deep loss engulfed her and she wept in agony, letting go all the emotions of fear, deceit, and disappointment that built up in the last few days. Moving her hands to her face, she couldn't stop the relentless tears overflowing from exhaustion and the reality that the harrowing experience had come to an end.

"There, there," Bradly said, dropping to his knees beside her and pulling her close.

She buried her head in his chest, sobbing so intensely that her body swayed with each burst of sorrow, and she couldn't catch her breath. As she felt her father rocking her back and forth, she began to feel calmer and began breathing again in short, gasping breaths.

"I didn't say good-bye," she whispered. "I don't even know where he's gone."

Bradly helped her to her feet and lifted her in his arms as if she were six years old. "We'll find him," he said. "Don't you worry about that."

Chapter 30

At the Templeton ranch, Bradly carried Sandy upstairs and laid her on the bed. "You rest a bit, now," he said, spreading a blanket over her.

"Dusty," she said, lifting herself from the bed. "I have to find Dusty."

"You just lie still. I'll find Dusty," he said giving the blanket a pat. "You rest a while. I'll take care of it."

She lay back on the pillow. "Thank you," she whispered.

Bradly left the room and hurried downstairs to the kitchen. "She'll be alright," he told Lily, who waited at the table.

She nodded as Bradly searched the telephone book." What's up now?" she asked.

"Sandy's worried about Dusty. I thought I'd just make a call to the Laramie hospital. I'm sure they took him there." He laid his finger on the number he found. "Here it is. This shouldn't take long. Sandy'll see everything's alright." He dialed the number and waited. "Yes, hello. I'm calling in reference to one of your patients." Listening a moment, he gazed at Lily. "His name? Dusty. His name is Dusty. Last name?" He searched Lily's face as she shook her head. "We just know him as Dusty." Bradly told the receptionist. He listened then covered the receiver. "There's no one with that name admitted," he told Lily.

"How many patients do they have who've been shot?" Lily asked in disgust.

Bradly nodded and turned his attention back to the phone. "He's been shot," he explained. "Do you have anyone admitted who's been shot?" Bradly waited nodding as he listened then hung up the receiver.

"They can't have many patients who've been shot," Lily said.

"She said they can't give out that information. They have to have his name," Bradly told her.

"Then we'll have to wait until Sandy wakes up. I'm sure she knows his proper name," Lily assured him. "Dusty's probably just a nickname."

"Yeah. Well, I'm going to get some work done," he said, grabbing his Stetson and heading for the door. "I'll see you around supper time."

Evening cast its long shadows across the Big Hollow when Sandy opened her eyes. She stretched and rubbed her swollen ankle then drew a hot bath and let the warm bubbled water wash away the dirt and grime from her Sapplehead experience. Lying back, she sighed and blew the bubbles clinging to her chin.

"It's as though all of it was a dream," she said then wiggled her foot. "No, more like a nightmare." She lifted her foot and examined her ankle. 'If that's all I suffered from it, I'm lucky." She returned her foot to the water's warmth then stiffened as the next thought flashed through her mind. "Dusty," she whispered. "I've got to find Dusty."

Quickly she dried, dressed, and rushed downstairs to the kitchen where Lily was preparing supper.

"Dusty," she said. "Did Dad call the hospital?"

"Oh, yes." Lily put the potato she was pealing in the sink. "Sit down. We ran into a little problem."

"What problem?" Sandy asked. "We don't really need any more problems."

"It's not a big difficulty," Lily said laying her hand on Sandy's. "Your father called, but they wouldn't give any information without Dusty's name. They don't have anyone named Dusty admitted." She patted Sandy's hand. "All you have to do is tell them his given name."

His given name. Sandy searched her memory. Although it hadn't been long since he told her, the time lapse could have been mistaken for years. Too much happened for her mind to save that information in its files and, as she covered her eyes to concentrate, all she remembered was something the Third. She shook her head in disgust.

"I can't remember. I wish I could look back to that first day at Vedauwoo when he told me his name, but on that ranch he was visiting, he was just called Dusty." She rubbed her head trying to inspire her memory to work.

"Maybe that ranch would know it. What was the name of the ranch?" Lily studied her anguished expression.

"I don't remember him ever saying the ranch's name. He was just somewhere in Colorado." She brightened as a new thought popped into her mind. "Maybe I could say I'm his wife."

"You'd still have to know his name. You couldn't just say you're Mrs. Dusty," Lily reminded her.

Sandy tapped the table and shook her head. "Then what shall I do?"

"All I can think of is, you'll have to wait until he calls you," Lily said as she returned to her potatoes.

"This is awful. I have to remember that name," she said. "He might never call because he thinks I don't care."

"I'm sure he doesn't think that," Lily assured her. "I could see he thought the world of you."

"I think I should drive to Laramie and demand to see him," Sandy said. "That's what I'll do. And maybe they'll show me the list of people admitted today. If I see Dusty's name, I'm sure I'll recognize it."

"I'm not sure they'll show you, but do what you have to," Lily said. "You can take your father's Oldsmobile. The keys are hanging there by the door."

Sandy nodded and studied the array of keys hanging on little pegs then recognized those that belonged to Sterling's Cadillac and slid them into her hand.

"I'm taking the Cadillac," she told Lily. "Dad did put gas in it didn't he?"

"Yes, he put a little in to get it to the house and he probably filled it, but you'd better check the gage, just to be sure. We don't want you running out of gas again."

"Okay," Sandy said, stepped outside and gazed at the dark car then opened the door and slipped in. The motor hummed as she turned the key and checked the gas gage. "Yes, Dad filled it. Now let's see if it can get me to Laramie."

The late afternoon shadows extended from the west when Sandy parked at the hospital parking lot. She hurried inside and, noticing a woman behind the reception desk, she tried to smile, but it appeared as a straight line across her face.

"Hello," she said. "I'm a friend of one of your patients that may have been admitted just a few hours ago." Excitement prevented her from sounding audible and she took a deep breath as the receptionist gazed thoughtfully at her.

"Are you alright?" she asked Sandy.

Without answering her, Sandy stammered on. "My friend was shot. I have to know how he is. Was anyone admitted who has a bullet wound?" She felt her hands shake as the receptionist checked her computer.

"And what is your friend's name?" came the baffling question.

Sandy wiped her sweating palms on her jeans and sighed. "I know him as Dusty. Can you just show me the names of those admitted with gunshot wounds? There can't be that many." She felt the negative response coming as the receptionist brought her attention back to Sandy.

"Well, we have two," she told Sandy.

"Two?" Sandy asked. "Are they here? Can I see them?"

"There's only one here now," the receptionist said gazing back at her computer. "One was flown to Denver."

"What about the one who is here? Is he young with blond hair?" Sandy began to get agitated with her and tapped on the desk.

"I don't know about blond hair, but the young one was sent to Denver." She smiled at Sandy. "He was admitted as Howard Davidson."

"The Third," Sandy finished her sentence. "Yes, Howard Davidson the Third. That's him. That's Dusty. I've found him." She felt all the clouds lifting as her heart pounded for another reason. A good reason. She felt as if she could sail across the ceiling when the receptionist handed her a slip of paper.

"Here's the phone number and name of the hospital. "I'd call before you travel down there."

"Why?" Sandy asked feeling the dark cloud forming again.

"It would just be a good idea." The lady at the desk smiled. "You go home and call before you think about traveling to Denver."

A cold chill starting at Sandy's feet traveled to her chest. "What is it you're not telling me? Dusty's alright, isn't he?"

"I don't know that," the lady said. "Just call first."

Sandy nodded. "Okay." She felt her legs getting weak as she hurried to the car, turned the key, and headed home as instructed.

"Why wouldn't she tell me?" Sandy asked as she drove down the edge of the Big Hollow. "You don't suppose he's dead?" She shook her head violently. "No, no, not that."

Chapter 31

Darkness slid across the Laramie Basin as Sandy stopped the Cadillac in front of the ranch house and hurried inside. Bradly and Lily sat at the kitchen table and Sandy knew they were waiting for her.

"What did you find out?" Bradly asked. "I couldn't get a thing out of them."

"He's not there. They flew him to Denver, but I did get his name and the hospital's phone number. I have to call and see if he's okay."

"And I'll fix you some supper," Lily said moving to the refrigerator.

"Nothing much," Sandy said as she lifted the phone's receiver.

"Just a sandwich," Lily protested. "You need something."

"Okay then," Sandy agreed as she dialed the hospital's number. Waiting patiently, she pushed the air from her lungs and rocked from her heels to her tiptoes. "Oh, hello," she said when she heard a voice on the other end of the line, then studied the note the receptionist at Laramie gave her. "I'd like to be connected with room three thirty six, please. Yes, thank you, I'll hold." Sandy felt her hand tremble and gave it a shake then gazed wide eyed at Bradly when she heard a woman's voice. "Hello, I'd like to speak to Dusty." She tried to stop saying that name, but Dusty was all that would slide from her tongue. "No," she said quickly. "Howard Davidson. I'd like to speak with Howard Davidson the Third."

"May I ask who is calling?" came the precise voice.

"Oh, I'm sorry. I'm Sandy Templeton. I'm a friend of his and I just have to know how he is."

"He's out of the room right now, but I'll tell him you called. What is your name again?"

"Sandy. I'm Sandy and who are you?" Sandy began to feel anger boiling in her chest.

"I'm his mother," came the voice through the line.

"Oh, I'm sorry I might have sounded curt, but Dusty-Howard," she corrected herself. "Howard and I have had quite an experience the last few days. He may have told you about it, if he's able to talk." Sandy shook her head at her own aggressive attitude toward this woman. "Will you tell me how he is?"

"He'll be just fine, but he lost a lot of blood after he was wounded in some wild place here in the west."

Sandy heard her grunt disgustedly and held the phone at arm's length as she blew the anger from her lungs and tried to speak softly. "Oh, yes. That place is Sapplehead," she said sweetly. Then more harshly. "And it's my place."

"So it is," Sandy heard the woman say rather snippily. "Howard will be ready to travel tomorrow, and we'll be going back home. He can recuperate very nicely there."

Sandy's heart skipped a beat. "Then he's going back to Chicago?"

"Yes, Chicago is our home," Mrs. Davidson said.

"Yes, of course," Sandy said as she pulled a chair close to the phone and wilted into it.

"And furthermore," Mrs. Davidson added. "This would never have happened if Howard had stayed in his office instead of galloping around like a cowboy. He has responsibilities and traipsing around the countryside with some girl is not one of them."

Sandy jumped to her feet and sent the chair tumbling over. "I am that girl, Mrs. Davidson and I'm not just some girl. I'm a schoolteacher and my father owns a ranch here in Wyoming." She stopped herself and bit her tongue knowing she was making matters worse. "I'm a friend of your son and I'm simply calling to find how he is." She waited, hearing only silence then it sounded like the woman was clearing her throat.

"I'm sorry," Mrs. Davidson finally said. "I'm just so upset. He could have been killed."

Sandy realized Mrs. Davidson's anger stemmed from deep concern for her son. "I'm sorry, too," Sandy said. "I was also worried about him."

"I thank you for your concern and I'm sure he'll be glad you called," Mrs. Davidson said.

Sandy nodded, realizing Mrs. Davidson was anxious to hang up. "Yes, please tell him I called," Sandy said. "And I hope to see him again sometime."

"Good bye," was all Mrs. Davidson replied then Sandy heard her hang up. Slowly Sandy returned the receiver to its cradle.

"He's alright," Sandy told Lily and Bradly. "That was his mother on the phone. She's taking him back to Chicago." She lifted the fallen chair and set it back on its legs. "I guess I'll not be seeing him again." She plopped onto the chair and wiped at tears forcing themselves down her cheeks.

"He'll be back," Lily said. "I'll bet you anything. That experience was too much for anyone to forget."

"You can count on it," Bradly assured her. "That boy's got a lot of good in him."

"He works in an office," Sandy said as Lily pushed the plate, holding a sandwich, toward her.

"We all work in different kinds of offices," Lily said. "Now, go on, eat the sandwich. Everything will be alright. Just you wait and see." She poured a glass of milk and sat it by the sandwich.

"By the way, Sandy," Bradly asked as he pulled his chair closer to her. "Did you find the brooch at Sapplehead?"

Sandy washed the bite with a swallow of milk. "No. I don't think it's there. The clue in the false brooch was wrong. There is no brooch at Sapplehead."

"That's strange." Bradly rubbed his chin. "I could have sworn the note meant you'd find it there."

"We looked everywhere it could possibly be," Sandy said putting the empty plate in the sink. "Someone else must have taken it. It just can't be found at Sapplehead."

"It wasn't in the tin box beneath the floor?" Lily asked. "He always kept his favorite things there."

"Only fishing stuff," Sandy said. "I think I'll go on to bed." Climbing the stairs slowly, she turned to their concerned expressions.

"It'll be alright," Lily said. "Just you wait and see."

Sandy nodded, but she didn't want to wait. And wait for what? She didn't find Grandfather's brooch and she lost Dusty. She turned down her covers on the bed and very roughly fluffed her pillows. She didn't think she liked Mrs. Davidson and expressed her disgust by punching the feathers. "She was very rude," she said as she slipped into her pajamas and lay beneath the sheet. "She did have good reason. I'm sure my mother would have acted the same way." She nestled her head into the feather pillow. "I wonder if Dusty has similar feelings for me as I do for him." She gazed at the ceiling. "Maybe he doesn't. We never talked about caring for each other. It just appeared that he more than liked me." She sat up, grabbed the pillow, and hugged it. "Sandy," she told herself. "You simply must get over it. He'll be home tomorrow and that will be the end of it." She replaced the pillow and plopped her head on it. "Oh, Dusty. Will I ever see you again?"

Chapter 32

June slipped into July and Sandy tried to forget Dusty. If he planned to call, he didn't, and she couldn't decide if she should call him after her discussion with his mother. She sat at the kitchen table and pushed her egg around the plate. The many activities she planned for the summer were no longer interesting. She couldn't conclude why but assumed they couldn't compare with the excitement she'd experienced with Dusty. She studied the list in her mind as she stabbed the egg yolk with her fork. Picnics with Jackie and her family and the Fourth of July celebration were on her list. She'd always loved seeing all the neighbors, playing dodge ball and badminton, watching the young people race their horses around the hollow, and resting on a blanket watching the summer clouds skim across the azure sky. It was all so wonderful before. Yes, it was wonderful before Dusty, but these paled in comparison to the time she spent with him.

"How about saddling your horse and riding with me to check the cattle at the west end of the Hollow?" Bradly asked. "It'll take your mind off things."

"That sounds good," Sandy said, feeling a spark of brightness.

"Well, finish your breakfast. You'll need it," Lily ordered. "That horse of yours hasn't been ridden for a while."

Sandy stopped abruptly in the middle of a bite. "What if Dusty calls."

"I'll take care of Dusty," Lily said. "You go see about your horse."

When Sandy finished eating, she met Bradly at the stables her grandfather just had to build. He hated to see his horses in the cold pasture during the winter.

"She might be a bit spooky at first," Bradly said, leading the mare." I haven't been on her for a while."

Sandy stepped to the stirrup and understood what Bradly was talking about. The mare moved from her as she attempted to board. Finally, the horse gazed at her, and Sandy knew the steed was pleased with herself, and Sandy was allowed to step into the saddle.

"There," she said. "I think I'm ready."

She followed her father west to the pine clad hills not far from Centennial. Eventually she found her seat on the rollicking horse and began to enjoy herself. Relaxing to the horse's gait helped her regain her composure in the saddle. Sighing, she realized she must relearn her riding craft every summer.

They found the cattle beside the stream that flowed from the high country. June's rushing waters now subsided to a calm sparking creak.

"There's someone fishing upstream," Sandy said as she stopped to let her mare drink.

"Oh, yes," Bradly said. "I would bet that's Danny catching his dinner. Let's go see how he'd doing."

They dismounted, allowing the horses to graze while they walked along the edge of the water.

"Hello there," Bradly called. "Are you catching anything?"

Danny hushed him as he drew in his line and tossed the fish onto the bank. "There, got him," Danny said. "Now you can talk. The fish don't like talkin' much." He laughed and held up the trout. "Would you like one? I got two of them."

"No, no," Bradly said. "I thought we'd eat lunch at the café in Centennial. Would you like to join us?"

"Sure," Danny said then studied them closely. "Did you guys walk from your place?"

Sandy giggled. "Oh, no. We rode horses."

"Oh," Danny said. "That's about as bad."

"We're heading to Centennial now. Would you like to meet us there?"

"I don't have to ride your horse, do I?" Danny asked.

"You can drive your pickup." Bradly gazed through the timber. "Wherever you parked it."

"It's just up there a bit," Danny said. "I don't like walkin' much or riding horses either."

"Alright then," Bradly said. "We'll get our horses and meet you there."

Danny nodded, removed his brown plaid Scotch cap, and rubbed his thick blond hair. "Yeah. I got something to tell you and Sandy."

"Whatever does he have to tell us?" Sandy asked as she climbed into her saddle.

"Beings it's Danny, I'd bet he has the cabin all cleaned up and he'll be wanting us to come and see his work," Bradly said, guiding his horse alongside hers. "Come on. Let's not keep him waiting."

Sandy tied the mare to a tree outside the café and followed her father inside. She studied the room then saw Danny sitting in a booth beside the window farthest from the door.

"I like to sit here," Danny told them as they sat opposite him. "I can watch the birds and animals and see who comes in the door."

"Have you ordered yet?" Bradly asked.

"Yeah. I did for all of us. Hamburgers all around," Danny said with a bit of pride and sat up straight in the booth. "I can do most anything now."

"That's good," Sandy said. "Now what did you want to tell us?"

Danny's gaze slipped to his lap followed by his hands, and he peered at them from his bowed head.

"I know what it is," Bradly said.

"You do? You really do?" Danny lifted his chin and smiled broadly.

"Sure," Bradly said. "You cleaned the cabin, and you want us to come see it."

"Yeah, I did that." Danny's smile slipped away, and he fidgeted in the booth. "It looks really good."

"I'm sure it does," Sandy said. "And we'll come see it as soon as we can."

"We have that Fourth of July celebration tomorrow. You'll be there, won't you?" Bradly said. "Of course, you will. You always come."

Sandy caught Danny staring at her. Cleaning the cabin wasn't what he wanted to tell them. She felt certain that stare meant something else.

"What is it, Danny?" she asked. "Is there something else?"

He paused and Sandy knew by his hesitation and those pleading blue eyes that the cleaned cabin was not on his mind.

"Yeah." Danny swallowed nervously and kept his gaze on her face. "That's all."

When the hamburgers arrived, Sandy noticed Danny ate slowly, gazing at her between each bite. When she finished, she pushed her plate aside. "Well, that tasted good," she said. "And I think we should take a trip to Sapplehead, but tomorrow you'll be coming to our Fourth of July picnic, you know. Maybe we can talk more then."

His face brightened and he nodded emphatically. "Yeah. Oh, yeah. That would be good. I'll be there tomorrow."

Sandy mounted her horse slowly as her thighs hurt from rubbing against the saddle. It would be a long trip home, but tomorrow she'd find out what Danny was hiding.

That night as she lay in bed, Sandy reviewed what Danny said at the Centennial Café. Perhaps she imagined his uncertainty to disclose what he actually wanted to say. Maybe it was her dad's presence that discouraged him. She didn't know but was eager to find out. If she went to Sapplehead alone, Danny might be more open, but that thought made her cringe. Too much had gone on at that cabin and she relived the experience every night in her dreams. No, she wanted someone with her on her return. Tossing and turning in her bed, she struggled with the decision. Realizing that she actually didn't want to go, she buried her head in the pillow. "I must face it sometime," she told herself. "Oh, Dusty, if you were only here." She fell into a fitful sleep and felt relieved when the summer sun peeked into her window.

Chapter 33

"Sandy, quick. Jump from that bed. You have a telephone call." Lily said as she opened Sandy's bedroom door. Her shining eyes and broad smile declared her excitement.

"Who is it?" Sandy asked as she grabbed her robe.

"You've been waiting a long time for it," Lily said without giving away her secret.

"Dusty," Sandy squealed. "It's Dusty, isn't it?"

"Yes, but hurry. It's long distance." Lily led the way downstairs, but Sandy passed her, rushed breathlessly to the kitchen, and picked up the receiver.

"Hello," she said, trying to catch her breath. "Dusty, is that you?"

"Yes," she heard him say. "I'm sorry I haven't called. I've been sort of busy."

Sandy patted her chest to quiet her drumming heart. "I'm glad you called," she said taking a deep breath. "Are you in Chicago?"

"No," Dusty said. "I'm in Laramie. I thought today would be a good time to drop in."

A good time to drop in. Sandy's breath reached her throat in tiny gasps. She covered the receiver and whispered to Lily. "He's coming. He's coming today."

"Sandy, are you there?" Dusty asked.

"Yes, oh, yes I'm here and please come."

"I'll be there shortly," Dusty said.

Sandy heard him hang up and replaced the receiver with shaking hands. She couldn't stop the tears that slipped down her cheeks and splashed on her chest. She wiped them away and hugged herself as she twirled around the kitchen.

"Did he say why he hadn't called?" Lily asked as she spooned her deviled egg mixture into the whites of the boiled eggs.

"He said he's been busy. That's all. But he's coming. He didn't forget." She sat at the table and sighed. "He didn't forget."

"I knew he couldn't," Lily said. "And he'll be here on an exciting day. We can all go to Jackie's together and have a wonderful time."

"Yes, a wonderful time," Sandy said. "Now, what can I do to help get ready?"

"You can start by eating some breakfast," Lily said as she put the deviled eggs into a plastic container.

"I couldn't eat a thing. Jackie will have a big bar be cue and there'll be plenty of food there." She wiped the last tear forming. "I can't believe he's coming today."

"You won't have the strength to talk with him if you don't eat something," Lily said as she put the eggs in the refrigerator.

"There's no room for food," Sandy chuckled. "There are too many butterflies in my stomach."

"Okay, then, but butterflies aren't very nutritious." Lily wiped her hands on her apron and reached out her arms. "I'm so glad he's coming."

Sandy jumped from the chair and welcomed the hug. "I'm glad, too. I hope he's alright."

"Well, I'd say, if he weren't, he wouldn't be on his way out here right now." She backed from Sandy and studied her. "But maybe you should wear something other than your pajamas and robe."

"Oh, yes," Sandy laughed. "I forgot I wasn't even dressed yet."

"Run along, then," Lily said. "Wear something pretty."

Racing upstairs, Sandy rummaged through her closet. Something pretty. She stopped at the peasant blouse and shook her head. "I'll get sunburned to my waist." Stopping at a soft cotton blue plaid with short sleeves, she nodded, pulled it from the hanger and slipped it on. "Now, what slacks?" She touched her lips as she thought. "Or should I wear a skirt?" Shaking her head, remembering the day's events, she stopped at a pair of light weight blue slacks. "Oh, yes, this will do fine," she decided.

Dressing quickly, she combed her hair and rubbed face cream on her cheeks. "There," she said, gazing in the mirror. "That's about all I can do with what I have."

As she hurried downstairs, she heard the knock and her heart banged inside the plaid shirt, but as she opened the door, Danny stood smiling at her.

"I'm here," he said. "Like your dad told me. I'm here." He wiped the toes of his shoes on his clean bib overalls.

Sandy smiled at his blonde hair slicked back from his shining face. "Come in," she said, and then stepped outside to check the road leading from the rim of the Big Hollow. When she saw nothing, she closed the door.

"It's Danny," she called to Lily.

"Come on in the kitchen, Danny," Lily called. "You can ride to Jackie's with us."

"Okay," Danny said and then stared into Sandy's face. "You have to go to Sapplehead. Not today, of course, because of the party, but you have to go to Sapplehead."

"Can you tell me right now?" Sandy asked, realizing the young man's anguish.

"I could, but you have to see and listen, and you'll know why I'm afraid." Danny wrung his hands and then wiped them on his jeans.

"You can't tell me now?" Sandy asked. "There's time right now before we go to the party."

"There's too much to tell. You have to be there and see and listen," Danny pleaded.

"I'll go tomorrow. How's that? Dusty, that fellow I was with when we stopped at Centennial will come along, too. I'm sure he will. We'll have everything settled tomorrow."

"That sounds good to have everything settled." Danny wiped his forehead. "Everything will be settled tomorrow." He nodded emphatically and strode to the kitchen.

Sandy gazed after him then opened the door and stepped outside. What Danny was afraid of, she couldn't venture a guess. He was a strange fellow and her father always said he was rather slow mentally, but that didn't have anything to do with his fear of something at Sapplehead. Whatever could it be? All the fearful people who had been there were gone. She shook her head and gazed at the road leading to the rim. Squinting, she studied the edge for a car bringing Dusty back to her. She sighed and shaded her eyes with her hand. A car appeared and she gasped, and then, as it passed on west, she groaned.

"He's coming," she said. "He said he was coming so he's coming." With her foot, she pushed at the stones in the driveway and stared at the rim again. At first she thought she saw only a dot then her heart leaped when she saw a small blue compact car turn from the highway and head down the road toward the Templeton Ranch.

"He's here," she whispered. "Oh, my dear, he's here."

Chapter 34

As the blue compact car stopped in front of the Templeton home, Sandy ran to meet its occupant. She pulled the car door before Dusty could open it and smiled at his familiar face.

"You came," she said, stepping back and trying to compose herself as he exited the car.

"Of course," Dusty said as he grabbed her with his right arm and drew her to his chest. "Was there any doubt?"

"Yes, actually there was for a time," she confessed. "I thought maybe you'd forgotten.

"Forget? I don't think I ever will," he chuckled.

Sandy stepped back and studied him from head to toe. "You look fine except for that sling you're wearing. Are you healing alright?"

"Oh, yes. It was a clean shot in my shoulder. The doctors said I'd be just fine so I decided to do some traveling."

"You didn't go to Chicago with your mother?" Sandy asked as she guided him to the house.

"No. Mom wasn't happy, but I had things to do."

Sandy stopped suddenly and gazed at him then at the car. "That's my car. You found my car." She left him standing by the door and hurried to the auto. "It is mine. It still has my stuff in the back seat. Where'd you find it?"

"It took some tracking," Dusty said following her to the car. "But I found it at that ranch where I was staying. The owner said he was sure someone would come for it."

"This is wonderful," she beamed. "You and my car came together." She took the keys from the ignition and opened the trunk. "Everything is here; my suitcase and everything."

"Your clothes might need some washing," he said. "Otherwise, I think you're good to go."

"Well, come inside," Sandy said, slipping her arm around his. "Lily will surely want you to eat something."

Lily did, and as he ate, he gazed around the familiar kitchen. "It's good to be back. It seems I haven't been here for a long time. Where's Bradly? Is he out doing his ranching?"

"No, he's at Jackie's helping them get the bar-be cue cooking," Lily said. "It's the Fourth of July, you know. We always have a big picnic up there every year."

"That sounds exciting," Dusty said as he noticed a figure standing slyly beside the cupboard. "I know you," Dusty said. "You work at that service station at Centennial."

Danny nodded and continued peering at him.

"This is Danny," Sandy said. "He takes care of Sapplehead."

Dusty left his meal and approached Danny, his hand outstretched in friendship. "Glad to see you again."

Danny smiled and nodded. "I remember you, too."

"Well, come sit down at the table," Dusty encouraged.

The smile continued as Danny sat beside Dusty and Lily brought the shy man a cup of coffee.

"Danny cleaned the cabin," Sandy said. "And he has something he wants to share with us at Sapplehead."

Dusty gazed at Sandy. "Something more at that place? It sounds pretty exciting." His gaze slipped back to Danny. "Is there more excitement at Sapplehead?"

"Yeah," Danny said as he relaxed toward Dusty's presence. "There's more." He drew a deep breath. "And kinda scary. You have to come and help Sandy get rid of the spook."

"Spooks?" Sandy asked. "Are there spooks up there?"

Danny nodded. "Yeah, there's a spook because of me."

Sandy gazed at Dusty, who shrugged and shook his head.

"What kind of spook?" Dusty asked. "We didn't see any spooks when we were there."

"There's one," Danny said. "And I caused it cause of what I did."

"There's a spook because you cleaned the cabin?" Sandy asked.

"No." Danny cringed. "Cause of what I did."

"What in the world would that be?" Lily asked as she poured more coffee. "You only do good things at that cabin. And as for ghosts, well," she smiled. "There would only be one."

"Yes," Danny said emphatically. "There's only that one."

"Grandpa," Sandy concluded. "You think Grandpa's spirit is at Sapplehead."

"It is," Danny said. "I'm sure of it."

"Have you seen this spirit?" Dusty asked. "I don't remember seeing anything like that." He gazed at Sandy. "Did you?"

Sandy shook her head and rubbed the goose bumps forming on her arm. "I don't think so. Unless he was the one who tripped Sterling by the tree." She rubbed her shoulders as the bumps climbed up her arm. "No, no," she finally said. "What are we saying? There's no spook at Sapplehead."

"Maybe we'd better go and take a look," Dusty said.

"There's something else, too," Danny said excitedly. "But you got to see it."

Sandy gazed from Dusty to Lily. "What do you think? Shall we forgo the picnic and go to Sapplehead instead?"

"Not go to the picnic?" Danny asked. "I really want to go to the picnic."

Sandy chuckled and patted Danny's shoulder. "Okay, Danny. We'll go to the picnic and go to Sapplehead tomorrow. Does that sound alright?"

"That's good," Danny grinned. "I like your picnics."

"Then it's settled," Dusty said. "Picnic today and we'll chase spooks tomorrow."

"Well, right now," Lily said. "We'd better get to Jackie's. There should be quite a crowd there by now."

Chapter 35

When they arrived at Jackie's patio, neighboring families were already milling around the tables. The deep scent of cooked beef filled the air as did the chatter and laughter of those attending. Children buzzed through the crowd squealing and giggling. Sandy felt friendly warmth from the familiar crowd and pulled Dusty into a line on one side of a long table laden with home cooked food.

She took a sturdy plastic plate and silverware Jackie brought from her picnic supplies and then surveyed the first table as she stepped in line behind Dusty. On the first table Sandy had to decide from all types of salads: fresh lettuce with tomatoes, cucumbers and onions, potato salads with onion, boiled eggs and one was warm with nuts and berries. Jell-O salads sat next with different fruits, cabbage with apples and nuts and several platters of deviled eggs. Sandy decided on the lettuce, Jell-O with bananas and, of course, Lily's deviled eggs. At the end of the table were platters of sliced fruit: apples, oranges, berries of every kind and sliced bananas. Trays of fresh vegetables sat next to the fruit.

On the next table Sandy had to decide among sliced ham, containers of fried chicken, a whole turkey, and casseroles with combinations of meat and pasta, some were tangy with generous amounts of chili. Next to these sat a large crock of baked beans. Breads of every kind hugged the bean container: homemade biscuits and rolls and thick slices of bread. At the end of the table Tom stood craving large pieces of bar be cued beef.

She spooned some baked beans and grabbed a chicken leg then let Tom plop a slice of beef on top of it all.

Sandy passed to the table holding drinks of lemonade, iced tea, and a large container of cool drinking water. She chose the iced tea and eyed the next table with deserts: pies, cakes, brown betties, and cobblers of all flavors. She shook her head, deciding she'd visit that table later.

Around the patio, blankets were laid on the thick green lawn and Sandy followed Dusty to one under the branches of a large cottonwood tree. She gently set the plate and cup down then sat cross legged beside Dusty.

"I don't think I've ever seen so much food in one place," Dusty said as he bit into the beef.

"It's like this every year," Sandy said. "Everyone brings something."

"I hope I can eat all this," Dusty laughed eyeing his plate heaped with food.

"You won't go away hungry," Sandy said as she tried the salads.

"Did I hear that games are played? How can you even move after a meal like this?" Dusty wondered.

"That's later. The youngsters participate mostly. They like to have horse races around the hollow." Sandy bit into a chicken leg and noticed Danny sitting with other young men. "Danny seems quite content with those young fellows," she said.

"It's puzzling why he's afraid up around the cabin." Dusty shook his head. "I wonder what it is."

"No telling with Danny. It could just be his imagination. I don't know." Sandy put her plate on the lawn and lay flat on the blanket. "I can't eat another bite and I did want some blueberry pie."

"Well," Dusty grinned. "I finish my meal and I think I will have some pie."

Sandy watched him stride to the desert table then laid back and observed the fluffy clouds of summer skim across the azure sky. "This is fine," she said "Everything is absolutely fine."

She heard Jackie call that it was time for games, but Sandy laid still and listened as the group took the remaining food indoors. Every year was identical: Grandma Lily washed dishes, another woman dried; Jackie slipped the silverware into the dish washer while the men set up tables in the living room for card games. She should get up and help, but her heavy eyelids refused to stay open. The yard and the patio area became quiet. Once in a while children ran by then the only sound Sandy heard were hungry flies buzzing around crumbs she dropped while eating.

She woke to the group talking and laughing as they brought the leftovers back to the outdoor tables. The sun shot wide streaks of light across the sky then pulled them back behind the timbered hills to the west. The badminton net was raised, and Sandy sat up and saw several young people batting the birdie back and forth. Further from the patio, teen age boys saddled their horses, lined them up and, yelling and laughing raced around the hollow.

Dusty stood at the table filling the paper plate provided with plastic utensils. He returned to the blanket beside Sandy.

"What happens now?" he asked.

"We eat and wait for darkness," Sandy said.

"That's not far away," Dusty said pointing to the sky. "Jackie turned the flood lights on so we could see what we're eating." He chewed on the piece of cold beef. "I don't think I've experienced such a day. It's really wonderful."

"I'm glad you like it," Sandy said as she pointed to the teen age boys returning and pushing each other to get to the tables first. They were allowed to fill their plates then the flood lights were turned off.

"Now watch the sky to the east," Sandy said.

The crowd sent out a single sigh as fireworks lit up the sky followed by loud pops.

"This is my favorite part," Sandy said.

Dusty put his arm around her. "Yeah, me too," he said.

"Well, tomorrow should be more exciting," she said as she pulled him close.

"This is great. I'm not used to excitement, you know," he chuckled.

She laughed and playfully hit his chest then laid her head against it. "That's about all we've had lately."

"I'm always up for more," he said. "I actually can't wait for tomorrow."

Chapter 36

Sandy stopped the four wheel drive pickup in front of the cabin. All seemed the same as it was before Sterling and Livingstone arrived. The pines were still deep green sending their spicy scent across the meadow. The Sapplehead pine waved to her with the west wind and the stream babbled playfully over the rocks in its bed. A jay screamed to another through the silence and Sandy sighed at her homecoming.

She stepped from the pickup smashing the tender meadow grass surrounding the cabin. "Are you coming?" she asked Dusty.

Reluctantly he followed her to the cabin door. "I don't know if I'm happy about this," he said as he jammed his hands into his hip pockets.

"I wonder where Danny is," she said as she surveyed the meadow.

"Is that his pickup coming up the road?" Dusty asked.

"Yes," she said as she recognized the old red vehicle.

"I guess it's time to become spook chasers," Dusty chuckled nervously.

Sandy nodded, but neither of them reached for the knob on the cabin door. "We'll wait for Danny," she said. "And we'll go in together."

"Good idea," Dusty said and kept his gaze on the approaching pickup.

Danny slowly stepped from his pickup and nodded to them. "Go on inside. See what I done."

Gently Sandy turned the knob, and her mouth formed a zero as she gazed around the cabin. "You fixed everything, Danny. This looks great. Better than before."

Danny swayed from one foot to the other. "Do you think your grandpa would like it?"

"Oh, yes," Sandy said inspecting the table, chairs, and the cupboard. "He'd be very proud."

"I had to do it good because of what I did." Danny lowered his gaze to his worn boots.

"Please tell us," Sandy said. "Sit down and tell us all about it. I'm sure Grandpa would want you to."

Danny nodded; sat on a kitchen chair he repaired and cleared his throat. "You see, I know where your grandpa put that pin."

"The brooch," Sandy clarified.

"Yeah. He said you would know where it was, but you wouldn't, you see, because I did a bad thing." He sighed and looked away from her. "He told me not to move it, but I had to, else the fire might get it."

"There was a fire?" Dusty asked, leaning closer to the conversation.

"Yeah, and he told me not to move it, but I did and now your grandpa's probably mad at me and wants to scare me." He wiped perspiration from his forehead and cleaned his shaking hands on his bib overalls. "He said you'd find it and you can't because I only know."

Sandy gazed into his frightened face. "I'm supposed to find it, but there's no way I'd know where it is." She moved her gaze to the bedroom as she thought of a plan to entice Danny into giving up his secret, then she nodded and gave Danny her whole attention. "What if I guess where it is? That wouldn't be telling me. I would be telling you and all you have to do is nod or shake your head. I'm sure that would be okay with Grandpa."

"Do you think so?" Danny narrowed his eyebrows thinking over her suggestion. "Yeah. I guess that'd be okay."

"Alright." Sandy put her fingers to her chin; hoping one of her guesses would be the right one. "We know it's not in the tin box under this floor, but, let's see. Sapplehead is the clue." She tapped herself on the head. "I know. That hole in the Sapplehead tree. That's where it is, isn't it?"

Danny slowly shook his head then volunteered an explanation. "The fire. I had to move it from there." Quickly he put his hand over his mouth and shook his head again.

"Then it was in that hole in the tree," Dusty concluded. "Why'd he put an expensive brooch in the hole in a tree?"

"Your grandpa was afraid those guys that used the cabin might steal it away," Danny volunteered again.

"So, it was in the tree? Now it isn't. It's not in the tin box under the floor." Sandy stopped, noticing a change in Danny's expression. Something she said made him giggle and his eyes brighten.

"Oh, ho," Dusty said. "I think we're making a breakthrough."

"What did I say?" Sandy shrugged. "I must have said something right."

"I think I know," Dusty said. "Under the floor. It's somewhere under the floor or under some floor, but not this one."

Danny nodded emphatically. "It's somewhere no one would look."

"Under the floor." Sandy studied the words. "Is it under the cabin floor somewhere?" She realized Danny was beginning to enjoy the guessing game as he giggled and shook his head.

"Let's see. What other floors are there?" She scratched her head visualizing the buildings on the meadow. "There's the tool shed. Is it under the tool shed?" Her shoulders slumped as Danny grinned and shook his head.

"There's only one other place left," Dusty said grimacing.

"The outhouse," Sandy said. "Is it under the floor in the outhouse?"

Danny brightened and nodded. "Gee, you're smart. Just like your grandpa said,"

"Well, let's go get that brooch from beneath the floor of the outhouse." As Sandy rose from her chair, she noticed Danny's expression become sullen again. "What is it?"

"Will it be okay now? Because I didn't tell where it was, and your grandpa won't be mad at me for moving it and telling where it is."

"You didn't tell me," Sandy smiled. "I guessed. It's like me finding it all by myself."

"Yeah. You found it by yourself." He nodded with satisfaction as he led the way to the outhouse.

Sandy opened the door then stepped back as the stench filled her nostrils. She allowed Danny to push by and she poked her head inside, holding her breath as he pulled a board from the corner of the floor and dug with his hand in the dirt below. She turned away when her lungs cried for a breath, and she sucked in the clean piney air outside the outhouse.

Danny's face beamed with pride when he brought out a small metal box, roughly soldered together. "I took awful good care of it. I made that box to protect it." He handed it to Sandy and backed away. "Now I don't need to be scared anymore."

"No," Sandy said as she gazed at the metal box the size of the palm of her hand. "You don't have to be afraid anymore."

Danny nodded and sighed in relief. "I'll be going now. I'm working at the filling station."

"Okay, Danny. Thank you. We'll probably be seeing you again." Sandy waved as he passed by in his pickup then brought all her attention to the box in her hand.

"I wonder if he welded it shut," Dusty said as he stepped closer for a better look.

Sandy lifted the heavy lid. "No, it opens easily."

Inside dirty cotton padding surrounded the patch of blue that Danny didn't securely cover. Carefully Sandy pulled the cotton away revealing a blue velvet box. She dropped the metal container, and her hands shook as she slowly opened the velvet case. She raised her eyebrows and her mouth uncontrollably opened wide.

"Wow, oh wow. Have you ever seen anything like this?" she asked as the red ruby winked at her as it caught the sunlight. "And look," she whispered. "It has that same lacy silver around it like the fake one." She removed it from the box and held it in the palm of her hand and gazed at Dusty to see his reaction.

His expression resembled hers as he blew the air from his lungs. "I think the word is exquisite," he said shaking his head in disbelief. "What now? Are we going to hide it away in some other outhouse?"

She smiled as she noticed the twinkle in his eyes. "I don't know. Now that I've seen it, the decision is difficult to make. Perhaps it should go back with the rest of the set in England."

"It's mighty pretty." Dusty shook his head again. "Unbelievable. I wonder what the British would say if they knew where it was stashed."

Sandy chuckled. "That's probably something they don't need to know."

She sighed as she sat behind the steering wheel of the four wheel drive. "It's over, Dusty. It's finally over."

Chapter 37

When Sandy and Dusty returned to the ranch, she showed the brooch to Lily and Bradly.

"Yes, I remember this," Lily said. "It lay in a drawer in the bedroom for years."

"What now?" Bradly asked. "What will you do with it? I'd suggest a safety deposit box instead of an outhouse."

"I'm thinking of returning it," Sandy said slowly. "I just don't know how to go about it."

"Give them a call," Bradly said. "Your grandpa has the number somewhere around here." He gazed at Lily. "Is that number in a drawer somewhere?"

Lily laughed. "Oh, no. It's in my address book. I'll get it."

Sandy called and the British relatives were only too happy to fly over and pick it up. Sandy gave her number and address in Colorado.

"I have to get back and do some planning before school starts," she said. "We have meetings and all kinds of boring stuff."

The next morning Sandy packed her things, put them in the trunk of the blue compact, and she and Dusty said their good-byes. Dusty drove to the Colorado ranch where he left his car and Sandy would continue on alone to Colorado Springs.

As they neared the ranch where Dusty stayed, Sandy felt an empty spot in her chest. "When will I see you again?" she asked.

"I have some work to do on the book I'm working on. I have an editor who's interested. I'll be back in Colorado after that."

"Did you get all the information you needed for your book on cowboys?" she asked.

"No. It's something different. The editor wants to see it finished and ready to publish next spring." Dusty said as he drove up to the ranch house. "I'll show you when it's published."

"You're not going to tell me what it's about, are you?" she teased.

"No, it's a surprise," he said stepping from the car and as the rancher and his wife appeared at their doorway, Dusty introduced her to them.

"I'm not for long good-byes," Dusty said as he drew her close. "But let me tell you, our experience was like a rocket to the moon."

"Then I won't see you again until spring?" Sandy hid her face in his chest.

"I promise I'll call you and when spring comes, there I'll be at your doorstep." He held her close. "I'm not going to lose you."

She felt his warm lips on hers then like the cowboys in the movies; he strode to his car and was gone.

Sandy sat on her couch and watched the robins pulling worms from the lawn outside her apartment in Colorado Springs. The winter seemed to last forever, but suddenly spring pushed it aside and life began again outside her window. She sighed at the slow passage of time and let her mind wander backward.

The English relatives had come, taken the brooch and left a sizeable check for its return. She thought about retiring, but one doesn't do that in their twenties. She sighed and gazed dreamily out the window then noticed a commotion outside. Someone was shouting.

"Get that thing off the sidewalk."

She left her seat to get a better look and felt her heart melt in her chest as she saw a man on a palomino horse.

"Dusty," she whispered as he waved to her from beneath his Stetson hat. Rushing down the stairs, she flung the door open and, as she approached, he caught her up onto the saddle.

"Shall we ride away together again?" he asked.

"Anywhere," she laughed. "But I have to be back to work on Monday.

"Here, take a look at this." He handed her a book and smiled over his shoulder.

"Sapplehead," she read. "You wrote our story about Sapplehead."

"It's all there. Everything and maybe a bit more." He winked and gave the horse a kick. "Well, shall we jump a fence or just ride off into the sunset?"

She hugged him tightly and whispered. "Wherever the horse will take us." She hung on as Dusty urged the horse down the sidewalk.

"I have a horse trailer down the block," he confessed. "I didn't ride from Chicago."

Sandy giggled and her heart swelled as she hugged him tighter. It was worth it, all of it. Those long days last June that seemed to last forever. She was suddenly grateful for Sterling, Livingstone and a cabin hidden away in the forest. A place called Sapplehead.

THE END

9 7 9 8 2 0 1 5 7 7 2 7 8